I hardly noticed as her hands slipped beneath my arms, still softly rubbing, and worked their way towards my breasts, cupping them in her palms and gently stroking them, caressing my firm nipples between her fingers. This felt even better, and my breath came in shorter and shorter gasps.

Then her right hand slid away from my right breast, gliding down across my ribs and over my waist, brushing lightly across my pubic hairs. That was when I opened my eyes, watching as one of Carole's fingers hesitantly probed into the top of my cleft. I twisted around quickly, and both of her hands fell away.

We were face to face, our breasts pressed against each other's. Carole's hands went around my waist, then dropped a few inches to rest on my buttocks. I gripped her wrists, and our eyes met. I let go, then tentatively I reached out to touch her, my right hand reaching for her shoulder, while my left touched her hip, feeling the hardness of bone beneath the supple flesh.

Slowly Carole's face moved towards mine, as her tongue darted out to moisten her upper lip.

We kissed.

My first kiss.

BLONDE

The stunning novel of strange sexuality.

Also available from Futura

BRUNETTE

Blonde

by

Anonymous

Futura
Macdonald & Co
London & Sydney

A Futura Book

First published in Great Britain in 1984
by Futura Publications, a Division of
Macdonald & Co (Publishers) Ltd
London & Sydney

ISBN 0 7088 2544 3

Typeset, printed and bound in Great Britain by
Hazell Watson & Viney Limited,
Member of the BPCC Group,
Aylesbury, Bucks

Futura Publications
A Division of
Macdonald & Co (Publishers) Ltd
Maxwell House
74 Worship Street
London EC2A 2EN
A BPCC plc Company

Chapter One

The only item of furniture in the room was the bed. It was a huge old four-poster, its black lace drapes drawn back and tied to the thick carved corner poles which supported the canopy. The mattress was covered by a black satin sheet, but there were no other bed clothes and no pillows.

John closed the door behind us, and I turned to face him. He was tall and slender, his hair a shock of thick black curls. He was wearing blue jeans, sleeveless green T-shirt and a pair of running shoes.

Neither of us spoke. There was no need for words. We knew exactly what we were here for and what we were going to do to each other. John put his arms around my waist, and his hands slid down to my buttocks as he pulled me against him. I raised my head slightly, my tongue coming out to meet his. My hands roved across his back, feeling his lean flesh, then stroking the taut muscles of his buttocks and thighs.

He ran his fingers through my hair, which is thick and wavy, long enough to hang down over the thrust of my breasts; and it's blonde, natural blonde.

My fingers eased themselves under the edge of his T-shirt and caressed the warm skin beneath, my nails digging in slightly as if to prevent him pulling away too soon. I held my left hand against his back, while my right explored the front of his torso, finding the web of hairs which covered his broad chest, then following them down, down, across his navel until the line of soft hairs vanished beneath his belt.

Bringing my left hand down as well, I unbuckled the thick leather belt and then undid the button which held the top of his jeans together. I slid his zip down with my left hand, while my right worked its way inside his shorts and found his cock. It was still curled up and felt small and soft in my hand, like a sleeping animal. But as my fingers closed around his balls, it began to awaken and come to life, stretching and growing.

Finally, reluctantly, I pulled my lips and tongue free from John's mouth. I wanted to see what he'd been hiding, the prize I now held in my grasp. John's arms released me from their tight grip, and his jeans tumbled to the floor and I pushed his yellow boxer shorts downwards. I let go of his prick, watching it grow and grow, springing up towards the vertical. Then I went down on my hands and knees in front of him to get a better view.

John's penis had seemed so small in my hand, but now its dimensions had increased amazingly. It was like John himself: long and slender . . . and hard.

Tucking my hair behind my ears, I leaned forward slightly as I took hold of his erection in one hand and guided it towards my eager mouth. My tongue darted out to lick the fullness of his proud flesh, and I could smell and taste the heady aroma of his maleness.

John simply stood there, accepting this as his due, although he pushed his hips forward, urging me to take him between my lips.

But I refused to be rushed. I licked for a moment, then pulled away, teasing him, squeezing him with my hand, just barely touching my fingernails against his sensitive skin. I wanted to let him know that it was my choice what I should give him – pleasure or pain.

I rolled his cock between the palms of both hands, then stroked his balls with my fingers as my tongue darted out again, almost touching him. Almost. John put his hands against the back of my head, trying to force me to swallow him; but in reply I pinched his testicles. Not much, not enough to hurt, but enough to remind him that what I did was up to me.

He got the idea, and instead he ran his fingers through my hair, rubbing the back of my neck. As a reward, I let my tongue caress his shaft, circling the swollen glans once or twice. Then I opened my lips wider, raised myself higher off the ground, and drew his penis into my mouth.

Only the first inch, which I then blew almost out again; but on the next breath I took in even more of his length; on the third breath I swallowed another couple of inches; and by the fourth gulp I'd taken as much as I could in a kneeling position. His cock filled my mouth, almost touching the back of my throat.

My lips worked on the outside of his organ, my tongue from the inside.

I felt John's hands moving down over my shoulders and onto my back, his fingers clutching at the flimsy fabric of my blouse. I was wearing a see-through top. But not for long. I heard a tearing sound as John ripped the back of my blouse from hem to collar.

I didn't let go of him even as he tugged at the front of the garment, raising it up and allowing my breasts to swing free and naked. He grabbed my right arm, bending it back at the elbow and pulling the sleeve off; then he did the same with my left arm. The ruined blouse dropped to the ground between us, and his hands reached down to cup my bare breasts, pressing the hard nipples against his palms.

He pushed off his running shoes with the soles of his feet, and stepped out of his jeans and underwear. I pulled my head away from his knob, all wet with my saliva, and wrapped my arms around his waist to haul myself upright. All John was now wearing was his T-shirt, and I helped him yank it off over his head. I stepped back, gazing in admiration at his lithe naked body for the first time.

The man moved towards me, but I raised my hand and held it against his chest. He could easily have brushed my arm aside had he wanted to, but instead he remained where he was. I pushed him back until his legs were touching the edge of the bed. He sat down, then shifted himself towards the centre of the mattress. He lay on the bed, putting his arms behind his neck, and he stared at me.

I tossed my hair back and ran my hands over my torso, stroking and rubbing my breasts, letting the nipples peek out from between my fingers. While my left hand continued to caress my boobs, I slid the fingers of my right beneath the waistband of my short white leather skirt. All the time I was watching John, watching him and his cock – both of them waiting for me.

I began to swing my hips from side to side as my hand moved further down, easing under the elastic of my black silk panties. My index finger crept over my pubic mound, and John could see exactly what I was doing. My shoulders started to sway, my head to nod up and down, and the whole upper half of my body was in motion; it was as if I was dancing without moving my feet. I withdrew my hand and raised my arms above my head, which had the advantage of lifting my breasts and showing them to their best advantage.

All I have to do is look in a mirror to remind myself what a good body I have. Though my breasts aren't large, neither are they small; they're firm and shapely and I don't need to wear a bra – and whenever I do the only reason is so that I can discard it at the appropriate moment.

I know I'm lucky to have such a great shape and physique, but I also take care of myself. I like to look good all the time, and there isn't a spare ounce of flesh around my waist or thighs.

At last my feet began to move as I danced slowly and sensuously around the foot of the bed, rubbing myself against the massive bedposts, gradually working my way to the side. John reached out, trying to grab hold of me, but I nimbly skipped aside and avoided his grasp.

My skirt was fastened by a row of buttons up my right hip. Without haste, one by one, I undid the buttons as I danced, starting at the hem and gradually working my way upwards, all the time displaying a greater and greater expanse of smooth ivory thigh. I'd have made a great stripper.

Eventually the skirt was held by a single button and I undid that one, letting the garment slide down but catching it before it fell too far, holding it between both hands in front of my hips, waving it from side to side, up and down, yet always keeping my skimpy silk briefs out of John's view.

I could see him becoming impatient. He wanted me now, immediately; but he also wanted to delay the moment, so that it would be all the more sweet when it arrived and I surrendered myself to him.

I used the leather skirt like a matador's cape, as a shield to cover my vulnerability. At last I twirled it around my head then flung it aside, and I became still. All I was wearing were my high-heeled white suede boots and my black panties.

Standing with my hands on my hips, I hooked my thumbs into the top of my undies, tugging first one side down a fraction of an inch, then the other. When the garment was half off, I pulled it back up again, as though I'd changed my mind, and I turned away. My back was to John, and also my bottom, the fabric hiked up tight between my buttocks like a G-string. I glanced over my shoulder, watching him, then I bent double from the waist, now seeing him upside down from between my legs.

Gradually, inch by inch, I thumbed down my briefs, twitching my hips from side to side. As I slowly stood up, I kicked the black silk aside. Then I spun around to face the man, wearing only my knee-high boots.

He had seen naked girls before, but probably never one as naked as I was. His eyebrows lifted and his eyes widened as he focused on my crotch – as nude as the rest of me, because I'd shaven off every one of my pubic hairs. John's mouth opened slightly, and he unconsciously licked his lips. He'd been lying on the

9

mattress a moment before, but now he was sitting up in readiness.

I was directly opposite him, and I raised my right foot and rested it on the edge of the bed, opening my legs to show him what I had to offer as I reached for the zip of my footwear. Removing the boot and casting it to the side, I lowered my leg – but not until I'd stroked the inside of my thigh, running my fingers right up to the secret line of pink where it met my other leg. Then I repeated the process as I shed my left boot, but this time I kept my foot on the bed and stepped up onto the satin sheet, taking two paces until I was standing astride John.

His head was directly below me, and he tilted his face upwards so that it was only an inch from my flesh. I could feel his warm breath on my skin, and as I glanced down I saw his exploring tongue stretch up and try to reach my cunt. I raised myself up, pulling out of reach for a second, then gently lowering myself towards his greedy mouth. I was already moist, my labia and clitoris swollen.

The touch of his tongue was like an electric shock shooting through my body, making every nerve tingle and pulse with fire. I rubbed my crotch across John's face, while his lips nuzzled the folds which hid my femininity and his tongue probed deep into its very centre.

I writhed with pleasure, moaned with delight. Very seldom do I have to fake it, and already I was building up in wave after wave which suddenly burst into the first ecstatic eruption of orgasm. Shuddering in helpless joy, I cried out as I experienced the first shattering climax.

John's mouth finally released me. I felt weak and drained as I slithered downwards against him, while he kissed my stomach, my navel, the firm pink tips of my breasts, my throat. He was guiding me onto his lap, and accurately I was impaled on his upright member. It felt so good to have him inside me, filling the emptiness between my legs. I was unable to move in any direction except up and down. His hands were on my breasts, expertly kneading and manipulating them, and a warm glow radiated from each of my nipples and flowed across the whole of my skin. John's hips jerked up and down slightly, driving his cock deeper within my vagina.

Taking the hint, I began to ride him, bending my knees back so that I was on my haunches and could get proper leverage. Using the internal muscles of my cunt, I tensed and pressured my flesh against his cock as it slid inside me, as though trying to grip his organ while I made my opening narrower and tighter.

John released my tits and put his arms behind him, pushing himself upwards and forwards, and then I was losing my balance and tumbling over and down onto my back. Our bodies stayed locked together, his prick embedded deep inside me.

And then he was above me, and I was lying on my back. Now he was in control; he held me pinned down, gripping my hands helplessly above my head. He drew his hips back, almost pulling his cock free, then thrust deep into me, harder and further than before. He did it again, and again, and again.

I opened my legs wide to allow him even more access, wrapping my thighs around his back. I reached down and around, taking hold of his balls in one hand, stroking his bottom with the other. Drawing my hand to my mouth, I sucked my index finger until it was nice and wet, then I probed between the cleft of his buttocks until I found the puckered edge of his anus. Carefully, I worked my finger inside.

John's eyes were clamped shut, his mouth open, his breath coming faster and faster in great ragged gasps as he gulped for air. We were both damp with glistening sweat, our bodies sticking together, squelching with every movement as we rocked to and fro. We worked as one, thrusting in unison, pulling back simultaneously.

11

Still drilling into me, John slowly raised his body away from the horizontal. He let go of my wrists, making me unlock my ankles from around his back and remove my exploring finger, and in a few seconds his torso was almost vertical. Then he pulled his prick free. I reached out, trying to catch his elusive cock, ready to take him into my mouth again, but he seized my arm and gestured with his head.

I knew what he meant, what he wanted, and I obeyed. Rolling over onto my front, I raised myself on all fours. John's left hand gripped my left shoulder, and I felt his right against my buttocks as he guided his tool towards its target. At first I thought he was planning to do with his dick what I'd done with my finger, but instead I felt his glans probing my inner labia and then he was back inside me again, taking me from the rear, fucking me as strongly as before.

Slowly, but surely, I could sense the tide welling up from the core of my being, taking me higher and higher. I hoped John wouldn't be through until he had guided me to the ultimate peak again. I could hear him breathing even faster now, feel his pulse racing and his heart pounding, and I knew that unless he could hold back it would soon be all over – and too soon for me.

He wasn't pushing so deeply now, or so powerfully; he was trying to restrain himself. I shifted my position slightly, ensuring that my clitoris was in better contact against his shaft. I didn't want to bring him off too fast, but neither did I want to lose what was so nearly mine. He seemed to realize what I needed, and one hand slid under me to fondle my tits while the other went to the aid of his cock, his fingertips expertly stroking my supersensitive cunt flesh.

I was breathing more quickly too, shoving my buttocks against his thighs, forgetting everything except the achievement of my desire. Another few seconds, that was all I needed. I started to cry out, gasping in sheer ecstasy, but only had enough breath left in my lungs to sigh with complete satisfaction.

Even then I wasn't through, because the sensation in my loins built up again, only more so. And my whole body exploded in a thundering series of overwhelming climaxes. One, two, three . . . I closed my eyes, losing count of how many times I moaned in unsurpassed and unsurpassable pleasure.

What brought me to my senses was John grabbing me by the waist and trying to turn me around. I'd been so lost in my amazing multiple orgasm that I hadn't even noticed his penis being pulled out of me. I opened my eyes, attempting to bring myself down and back to total awareness.

John was holding his cock in one hand as I turned to face him, and we were kneeling opposite each other. I glanced into his eyes, and he nodded almost imperceptibly.

I leaned back, lying on my side, supporting myself on my left elbow. John approached me. He let go of his tool; I accepted it in my right hand, pulling him even closer. As his prick came in range, I thrust out my tongue, licking at his testicles. They had hung loose previously, but now they were together in a tight sack. I pointed the purple tip of his cock towards my face, stroking it up and down in my hand. It was damp and sticky.

Opening my mouth, I drew the swollen glans between my lips, alternately sucking and gently nibbling with my teeth. I tasted both sperm and cunt juice, a sensational mixture of the world's most powerful aphrodisiacs. Greedily, I devoured his glorious prick.

After a few seconds I felt a change in the rhythm of the flesh sliding between my lips – a tremor which came from within, not from John's efforts to shove it even further into my mouth. I knew at once what this meant, and I pulled back my head just as the first creamy jet of spunk fountained from John's member and splattered against the side of my face.

13

I took a better aim and directed his jerking cock towards my mouth, catching the second spurt on my top lip before taking the next one into my mouth. His prick pulsed time after time, shooting his warm sperm towards me. I licked hungrily at the end of his dick, making sure I didn't lose any of the vital fluid, then my tongue caught the drops which hung thickly from my lips.

Wiping at my cheek where he'd first come, I sucked each fingertip in turn until every last atom of semen was in my mouth or down my throat. My eyes were closed, and I sighed contentedly. I sat up, running my hands across my breasts then down over my ribs and to my hips.

Opening my eyes, I flicked my hair back over my shoulders, twisted around and swung my legs off the edge of the bed. I looked at Mark.

'That was great, darling, marvellous,' said the director. He nodded and smiled at me. 'That's fine everyone,' he continued. 'Thanks.'

The two cameramen put down their video equipment; the lighting engineer pulled the plug and the battery of lamps was extinguished; the sound man removed his earphones and switched off his tape recorder. More sound would be added to the finished version, some dialogue being looped into the track. The tape from both cameras would be edited together, so that the final film would show all the best angles in detailed close-up.

Mark was the best director in the game, and he always worked with the best team. And that of course included me – the star of the show.

Mark was about thirty, although he looked older. His hair was thinning, but to make up for it his waistline seemed to thicken every week. I'd worked with him numerous times by now, and he'd long ago discovered that he didn't have to 'direct' me. If he left me to behave instinctively, to act out my own erotic fantasies, then he'd wind up with the ideal video porn. All he

14

had to do was make sure the cameras were pointing in the right direction and provide the set plus an appropriate number of fellow performers, either male or female . . . or male and female.

'Good work,' Mark said, moving his attention to John.

I hadn't met John until this afternoon, and I'd probably never run across him again. Certainly I'd never work with him again. I'd fucked him once, and that was enough, because there were so many other cocks in the world to try. John had been competent, but nothing exceptional. He was there for only one reason – the director and his audience wanted a few inches of meat, and John was it.

And I'd wanted a stud too – but then I usually did. I was very fortunate, I knew: I was paid for doing what I liked to do more than anything else.

'Thanks,' John replied. Now that it was all over, he seemed embarrassed. He was sitting with his hands covering his limp penis. But no one was taking any notice of him. The technicians were packing away their gear, Mark was looking at me. No one was interested in John.

The director came to sit on the edge of the bed by my side.

'How are you fixed for the day after tomorrow?' he asked. He was staring me in the face, but having trouble keeping his eyes on the same level as mine. I turned towards him, my breasts swaying. As though unaware of what I was doing, I stroked my left nipple across his bare arm, below the rolled-up sleeve.

I was always teasing Mark like this, and he always did his best to ignore me. When we'd made our first film together, I thought it wouldn't do my career prospects any harm if I made myself available to the director – but Mark didn't want to know.

'I never mix business and pleasure,' he'd told me icily as I tried to undo his pants zip with my teeth. I'd since discovered that Mark was happily married to his

15

childhood sweetheart. They had numerous children, and he'd never screwed anyone else but her.

He made some of the best short sex films in the world, but he treated the whole thing as though he was running some other business – like he was dealing in frozen vegetables or bulk concrete, or something like that. I'd never once noticed the telltale bulge of an erection inside his trousers, though usually the rest of the crew had hard-ons which rivalled the male stars'. Frequently one of the technicians would have to act as a double, paid a bonus for the use of his erection, when the leading man had shot his load too soon or had only been able to dribble a few miserable drops from the end of his cock.

'Day after tomorrow?' I repeated. I shrugged, which set my tits jiggling. 'Nothing so far as I know. What have you got planned?'

I rose and picked up my discarded silk panties, giving them a shake. Turning to face Mark, I wriggled into the garment, tugging it snugly against my crotch.

Mark kept his eyes on my face. 'I've got the use of a railway carriage from a feature movie,' he explained. 'You play a girl who can't find her ticket when the inspector boards the train. You strip off, searching for the ticket but still can't find it.' He shrugged. 'So you pay your fare in a different way. The inspector, the guard, maybe even the driver – so we can finish on a comic note with the train jumping the rails and crashing.'

John had been listening. As the film crew carried the last of their equipment out and vanished, he spoke up. 'Would there be a part in that for me?' he asked.

Mark didn't bother to look around. 'Put your clothes on, kid,' he told him.

John did as he was told. They were his outdoor clothes, whereas some of mine had been brought along especially for the film.

That reminded me, and I picked up my ruined blouse from the floor. I supposed that I couldn't really

16

blame John for getting over-excited and ripping it from my body, but it hadn't been cheap.

Mark had pulled out his wallet and was counting a few banknotes onto the bed. Then he saw my shredded see-through, and he picked up half the pile again. He pointed to the remaining money on the mattress. It was as if he didn't want to hand it to John directly for fear of being contaminated.

'You should be more careful with other people's things, kid,' Mark said.

John finished dressing and picked up the money. He frowned as he studied his pay, but then he stuffed it into his back pocket. He looked at me and half smiled. I was expecting him to come out with one of the usual remarks: to say he'd have fucked me for free, or maybe even to ask me what I was doing that evening. But when I kept my face expressionless, he simply turned and walked towards the door.

'Well,' he said, 'goodbye . . .'

Neither of us replied, and he went out.

'Here's your expenses,' Mark told me, offering the notes he'd deducted from John's stud fee.

I took them, picked up my boots and skirt, and made my way towards the door. I'd left my other clothes in the next room along the hall. We were shooting in a house Mark had borrowed from a friend – that was where most of his locations seemed to come from.

'How much for next time?' I asked him, as he followed me out.

'Same as this,' he said. 'Not bad for a few minutes' work.'

In the other room I pulled my tight fluffy turquoise sweater over my head before squeezing into my even tighter jeans, tucking them inside the white suede boots.

'I think it's time for a pay rise,' I said. 'I'm worth it, we both know that.'

Mark nodded reluctantly. 'I'll see what I can arrange.'

'Thanks, Mark,' I said, and he allowed me a swift kiss on the side of his face.

'Here you are.' The man gave me an envelope.

I pretended to weigh it in my hand, then opened my quilted bag and dropped it inside next to the leather skirt. I didn't have to count it, the right amount was always there. Mark was an honest trader; he cheated neither his suppliers nor his customers.

I snapped the brass clasp shut, thinking about the money. As Mark had said, it wasn't bad for a few minutes' work – and though once I might have done it for free, not any more. What was the point of giving it away? That was for idiots and amateurs. It was like working for nothing. I'd always been given the proper rate for the job, and no one had ever tricked me and got away with it.

It had all started when I was five years old. His name was Tommy, and he must have been three or four years older than me. He offered me a handful of pennies if I'd lift my dress and pull down my drawers. It seemed like a good offer, and so I did what he requested. I don't know what he expected but he was very disappointed.

Even after so many years, I can still recall his words of complaint: 'But there's nothing there. I'm not paying you for that.'

Or at least such was his intention. But I grabbed hold of his hand and sank my teeth deep into his thumb, causing him to scream in pain. And I didn't let go until he'd filled my other hand with the promised coins.

Chapter Two

I used to hate men, or rather boys. My first love was for horses, and my second was Carole.

Boys were rough and rude, only interested in fighting and football and pulling my hair at school. I was an only child, a lonely child, and I had no real friends until I met Carole. I got to know her through the riding school where we both went. She was a year older than me, and I must have been about thirteen when I first met her. Over the next couple of years we became close friends. We'd go shopping together, buying clothes or records, then I'd go to her house or she'd come to mine so that we could play our new discs.

Most girls of our age were getting involved with boys, but we preferred to keep the opposite sex at a safe distance – as pop star pin-ups in magazines, as posters on our bedroom walls.

But what we had most in common was our passion for horses. When I look back now, the attraction of riding seems so obvious that I'd be embarrassed about climbing onto a horse nowadays. It's become a sexual cliché: the image of a girl on horseback, in her severe riding uniform of helmet, jacket, jodhpurs and leather boots, with the riding crop in one gloved hand, holding the reins in the other. But it's a cliché because it's true – sitting high in the saddle, legs wide open with a powerful animal between them who will do your bidding with a touch of the reins or whip. The smell of the leather, of the sweating horse. And the rhythm of the beast moving beneath the rider as they trot or gallop along together . . .

It's no wonder girls have such a fondness for horses and riding. I must have experienced my first orgasm on horseback – and never realized it! Of course at that time I'd no idea what an orgasm was. Even at fifteen I was very naïve and innocent.

I often spent the night at Carole's house, and she would come and stay at mine even though we only lived two miles from each other. Carole had an elder brother, but he was away at college. Then one weekend Carole's parents had to go away for some reason, and instead of her coming to stay with me we managed to persuade our folks to let us stop together at Carole's house. We saw it as some grand adventure, being all alone in the house. Our parents agreed. They knew we weren't going to be throwing any wild parties and wrecking the house – because we didn't have any friends to invite even if we did want to hold some kind of teenage mass orgy.

My main fear was that I'd be kept awake all night, scared of the dark because of some spooky horror story Carole had told me. That had happened the previous time, when she'd been staying at my house. Carole had invented such an awful tale, of ghosts and ghouls, that she'd frightened herself too and we'd kept the light on in my room all night.

Carole was a good looking girl, tall and slim, with jet black hair which fell in natural ringlets. I remember envying her, because I always thought of myself as small, plain and fat – although when I see photographs of myself I wonder what gave me that idea. It must have been a lack of self-confidence, I suppose. And also I was a late developer, stretching and growing out of my puppy fat after most of my contemporaries.

And in those days I hated my blonde hair, because it made me so distinctive and I always felt that everyone was looking at me – but now I'm disappointed if everyone doesn't look at me!

Carole phoned me up on the Saturday morning to say her parents had left and ask when I'd be arriving and to bring some records over for the evening. My bag was already packed full of clothes even though I'd only be spending one night away from home; but a lot of it was my riding gear, as I'd be going straight to the stables with Carole on Sunday morning. I sorted through my record collection and filled another bag. I strapped the first one to the back of my bicycle, and held the other one across the handlebars as I cycled to my friend's house.

When I rode through the open gate at the end of the drive, I noticed her watching from the front window.

'Hi,' she greeted me, smiling, coming out of the door as I left my bike inside the garage.

'Hi,' I said, unbuckling my bag, grinning at her.

We took my bags and went inside.

'Well,' said Carole, 'here we are then.'

I nodded, and we looked at each other.

'Tea or coffee?' she asked.

I couldn't make up my mind. 'I'm not sure,' I told her.

'I know,' she said, and she laughed. 'We'll have both!'

And so she made two cups of tea and two cups of coffee, and we sat in the kitchen giggling as we drank them.

'Now what?' asked Carole.

'I don't know,' I said, shrugging, and we both sat there wondering what to do.

'How about lunch?' Carole suggested.

'Okay.'

By the time we'd raided the freezer and heated up something, then eaten it and done the washing up, it was still only noon. It looked like it was going to be a long weekend.

We went into town during the afternoon, listening to the latest sounds in the record store, then trying on lots of clothes in all the boutiques. We didn't buy anything, of course. But by that time we were feeling hungry again, and we each had a hamburger and milk shake. Then we decided to go and see a film.

There was one cinema, but it offered a choice of three programmes. The first was a Walt Disney cartoon,

21

which my parents had originally taken me to ten years before; the second was a Western – and if there's anything I hate it's a Western; the third was a sex film.

'We can't see that,' I said.

'Why not?' Carole asked.

'We're not old enough. You have to be eighteen to get in.'

She nodded thoughtfully. 'But I'd like to see the film, wouldn't you?'

I sipped at my drink, not answering, because I wasn't sure that I did want to see it.

'Have you ever seen a sex film?' Carole wanted to know, and one glance gave her the answer. 'Me neither,' she added. 'But I think we ought to, don't you?' She bit her lip, trying to suppress a smile, her eyes wide with daring.

'Okay,' I agreed reluctantly. 'But how do we get in?'

'Don't worry. I'll buy the tickets, because I could pass for eighteen, and you stay in the background.'

'What if they won't let us in?'

'Nothing ventured, nothing gained,' Carole said. 'They can only say no, can't they?'

I nodded. Trying to get into a cinema wasn't a criminal offence, as far as I knew.

So we went over the road and pushed in through the glass swing doors. I stood looking at the poster for the Walt Disney film while Carole bought the tickets. Then we went inside. It was as simple as that. No one took any notice of us. I suppose they were glad to sell their tickets and didn't care who came in so long as they paid.

I think it was probably the worst film I've ever seen in my life, although I can't remember what the title was or even much about the plot – not that I think there was much of one. It seems odd now, but I recall being embarrassed by what I saw and glad it was so dark inside that my blushes couldn't be seen.

And it was all so harmless. Just a few naked bodies, male and female, and simulated sex – but as I'd never

22

seen any naked bodies before and didn't know much about sex, the whole thing shocked me. The men were only briefly seen in the nude, and there was certainly no such thing as a penis in the functional position. I spent more time looking down at the floor than at the screen, though I was careful not to close my eyes in case Carole should notice.

But she was totally engrossed in what was happening, staring up at the screen as she filled her mouth with popcorn. When it was at last all over, she simply sat there and for a minute I thought she intended to stay for the next performance.

Carole turned to look at me. 'That wasn't much good, was it?' she said, rising to her feet. 'I think we ought to ask for our money back.' She shook her head in disgust.

I kept my head bowed as we walked out, because the lights were up now and I didn't want anyone to see me. There might be someone in the audience who recognized me and would tell my parents where I'd been. It didn't occur to me that even if someone did know me, they weren't going to admit that they'd been to view a sex movie. Sex movie! What a joke that seems now.

We took the bus back to Carole's house, but neither of us mentioned the film during the journey. When we got back, we went up to her bedroom to play records. I was sorting through the collection, and Carole had disappeared. When she returned, she was carrying a tray with two glasses.

'Thanks,' I said, accepting one of them and staring at the contents. It was colourless, with an ice cube floating at the top; it looked just like a glass of water. 'What is it?'

'Try it,' Carole told me.

I did. It was sweet and fizzy, and I drank half of it in a single gulp.

'It's vodka,' Carole said.

I stared at her. I'd tried alcohol before, although I'd never liked it at all; but this tasted quite good to me.

'With lots of lemonade,' she added. She took a mouthful of her own drink. 'Like it?'

I shrugged. 'It's okay.'

'We can try something else later. There's whisky and gin and brandy and rum, and all sorts of liqueurs – they're the nicest of the lot really. You have to add too much lemonade to the others to take away the awful taste.'

Carole sat on the bed while I chose an album and put it on her stereo. I sat down next to her, and she nodded in approval at my choice. We talked about the music and made a promise that we'd go and see the group next time they gave a concert in our area. Then Carole turned the conversation towards the film, although I'd been trying to forget it.

'I was very disappointed,' she said. 'I thought there'd be a lot more to it than that. You know what I mean?'

I nodded, although I wasn't too certain. There'd been more than enough of everything for me.

'We hardly saw any naked men at all,' she complained. 'It was all boobs and hairies. That's okay if you're a man, I suppose.' Carole took a gulp of her drink, swilling the ice cube around so that it clinked against the side of the glass. 'Don't they make sex films for girls to look at? Ones with lots of men's thingies.' She turned to look at me. 'Have you ever seen one, you know, a stiff one?'

My jaw dropped in surprise at her question, and all I could do was shake my head.

'Me neither,' said Carole. 'Aren't you curious? I am. I thought we might see one in the film, but no such luck. And they weren't even fucking, were they?'

I stared at her, amazed by the word she'd used. I'd only ever heard it said by some of the boys at school. I knew what it meant, of course, but to actually hear Carole come out with it really threw me. It was so unexpected, totally unlike her.

Carole was watching me, studying my reaction, and I realized that she'd just been trying to shock me – and she'd certainly succeeded. I tried to be casual as I spoke.

'Who cares about . . . fucking?' I said, speaking the word for the first time ever. I shuddered. 'The idea gives me the creeps.' I'd never let anyone do that to me. Men were horrid smelly creatures, and none of them was ever going to even touch me.

'I know what you mean,' Carole agreed. 'It's hard to believe that people really do it, isn't it?' She drained her glass, still watching me. 'Imagine having some boy stick his thing into your cunt.'

I pulled a face, to mask my increased surprise. 'I'd prefer not to imagine it,' I said, then gulped at my own drink.

'I've seen horses do it,' Carole continued. 'And dogs. It all seems pretty disgusting, doesn't it? When we had our sex education lessons, it almost made me sick.'

My reaction hadn't been quite that extreme, but I simply hadn't believed the teacher. It seemed so ridiculous. Why would people ever want to do such a thing? The idea was so strange and repulsive that it was a wonder the human race hadn't become extinct by now.

Carole seemed to share my opinion, but she was about the only person I knew who did. Most of the girls in my class had boyfriends, and one even had to leave school because she was having a baby. They used to boast to each other about what they'd done to their boys, or where they'd been touched, and show off their love bites – opening their blouses to reveal purple marks on the top of their breasts, or even pulling up their skirts to display red passionate weals on the inside of their thighs.

'Want another drink?' Carole asked, and I nodded.

While she was gone, I picked up the album cover and tried to imagine what the guys in the group looked like without their clothes. Men were so ugly in the nude, that grotesque sausage of flesh hanging down as though it didn't belong to them. It was obscene, that was the word for it. At least girls kept their sex parts decently hidden away. Until that film I'd never seen a real man totally starkers, although I'd looked at paintings and statues – never a photograph of the genuine article.

But I had seen one in the flesh, so to speak. There was a boy in my previous class who had sat in the back row in the desk next to mine, and every now and then he'd unzip his pants and pull out his thing and point it at me. He was a horrible overweight boy, and his dick was like a fat slug. I always tried not to look at it, and he only did it to annoy me. At least he'd never had an erection, although that was probably what he'd been trying to achieve – by watching me as he stroked and played with his thing.

I'd preferred to look at the girls in the film rather than the men. The naked women had been so perfect, with their lovely bodies and smooth flawless flesh – while the men had simply looked silly. It was easy to understand why men liked seeing pictures of nude women – and obvious why girls didn't get turned on by naked men.

Who needed men, anyway? What good were they?

Carole returned eventually with another drink. I wasn't sure what it was, and didn't ask – I simply drank it down while I ate the cheese and crackers that she'd also brought up with her.

We drank and talked and ate and laughed then drank some more.

'Have you ever had a boyfriend?' Carole wanted to know, turning the subject back to our earlier conversation.

'Not really,' I said.

'Not really? What does that mean? You either have or haven't.'

'Well . . . I suppose . . . I haven't.'

A few boys in the senior classes had asked me out,

but I'd always turned them down. There was something about the male of the species which I totally detested. I'd felt this way ever since I was a child, so it couldn't have had anything to do with the theory of physical sex. Looking back, I've no idea what it was. All I know is that I was absolutely wrong, and I wish I hadn't wasted so much of my life avoiding men – but I've tried to make up for it since!

'What about you?' I asked.

'Not likely! It was my brother's friends who put me off. Coming around here, all sweaty and stinking, then being sick because they've had too much to drink.' Carole paused, glancing at the glass in her hand, then she shrugged. 'And the stories they used to tell about their girlfriends, the way they laughed about them behind their backs and treated them like slaves.' She shuddered. 'I prefer horses.'

'Me too,' I said, and we raised our glasses in an equine toast.

'And I'd much rather talk to a girl than some stupid boy. They're all so immature.'

I nodded, then wished I hadn't, because the room seemed to spin around. I couldn't understand it until I lifted my glass to my mouth – and missed, spilling the cold liquid down my chin. Then I giggled uncontrollably, because I realized what was wrong – I was drunk! Not that there was anything wrong about it, quite the opposite in fact. It felt very nice.

Carole was watching me with a puzzled expression, then my laughter infected her and she also began to giggle, not knowing why, but greatly amused simply because I was.

We were sitting side by side on the bed, leaning against the wall, and we laughed and laughed, rolling about helplessly as we fed each other's hysteria. We kept bumping into one another, and I elbowed Carole lightly in the ribs while she slapped my knees, and then she put her hand on my shoulder, and I could feel the warmth of her fingers. I became silent immediately,

27

looking at her smiling face a few inches away from mine, at her moist lips . . .

And Carole stared at me, as our eyes met. Then I turned my head away quickly.

'Shall I put another record on?' I suggested. I didn't wait for an answer, sliding off the bed, Carole's fingers releasing me from their grip.

Carole brushed a stray hair across her forehead. 'Yeah,' she said after a second. 'Go ahead.'

I changed the album, then returned to the bed. I sat further away this time, and neither of us spoke for a few minutes.

'Do you want another drink?' Carole asked.

'No thanks.'

'Me neither.'

Gradually we started talking again, this time about things like school and riding and music. The record ended, and I turned it over; the second side finished, and Carole chose the next selection. When she turned around, she noticed me yawning.

'It makes you tired, doesn't it, this drinking?' she remarked, glancing at her watch. 'Maybe we ought to think about hitting the sack.'

It wasn't very late, but I did feel tired. It had been a fairly busy day – cycling and shopping and the movies. And there'd be no Sunday lie-in tomorrow because we had to go riding.

'That's right,' I said, and I glanced over to the folding bed which stood against the far wall. There was a spare room, her brother's room, which he only used during the college holidays. But I always stayed in Carole's room, so that we could keep on talking even after we'd gone to bed.

'Do you want anything else to eat, some supper?' Carole asked.

'No thanks.'

She glanced at her empty glass, then smiled. 'How about a nightcap? That's the right word, isn't it?'

'No thanks.'

Carole shrugged. 'Okay.' She climbed off the bed, stretching. 'Do you want the bathroom first?'

'No, you have it.'

She nodded, reaching under the pillow for her night dress, then left the room. I collected the glasses and plates, the remains of our snack, and carried it all downstairs to the kitchen. I put what was left of the cheese and crackers back in the fridge and cupboard before washing up the handful of dishes. When I returned to the bedroom, I unfolded my bed and made it up with the sheets and blankets which had been left out for me. Then I unpacked my bag, taking out my toothbrush and towel and pyjamas.

Carole was still in the bathroom. She always took ages in there. I went to stand outside, and I could hear the water running. It sounded as though she was having a shower.

Back in the bedroom, I closed the door and quickly undressed, putting on my pyjamas. Then I sat on my bed, flicking through a magazine and waiting.

But after a few minutes, when it seemed as though Carole was going to be in there forever, I walked to the bathroom and tapped on the door.

'Will you be long?' I asked.

'No,' Carole replied. 'Come in if you want, the door's unlocked.'

So I opened the door and went in. The room was full of steam. Carole was standing in the shower, the curtain drawn open.

She was naked.

Chapter Three

I stared at Carole, unable to move – not wanting to look at her, but fascinated by the sight of her nude body, all pink and soapy.

And she looked at me, her right hand caressing the sponge to her left breast. Water dripped from the black curls of her head and those between her legs.

Carole was the first naked girl I'd ever seen. I'd seen photographs in the magazines the boys had at school, and there had been that film a few hours earlier. But apart from my own mirror image, I had never seen another nude female.

My heart had started beating faster as soon as I saw Carole, and I felt a strange stirring in my groin. My nipples had become instantly hard, pressing against the fabric of my pyjama jacket.

But I couldn't stay there, I had to leave. It wasn't right for me to be in here. Why had Carole invited me in? Why had she left the door unlocked?

She didn't seem at all concerned that I was watching her. In fact, I suddenly realized, this was exactly what she wanted!

I'd so often admired the girl's figure, but she looked even more stunning in the nude. Then I closed my eyes for a second, trying to blank out that thought, not to see her, to turn and leave the bathroom.

'Wash my back for me, will you?' Carole asked. 'It's hard to reach.'

Not wanting to, yet at the same time unable to refuse, I stepped towards her. The shower was switched off, and Carole turned her back to me – and also the superb curves of her glistening bottom. She held out the sponge to me, and I accepted it.

As if in a dream I began to soap her back, my hand

making circles on her skin – while my fingers kept touching her warm flesh.

'Ahhhhh,' Carole murmured. 'That's wonderful. Don't stop. That's it. Harder. Just there. Now lower down.' Her muscles tensed and relaxed as I sponged her, while my fingers obeyed her commands, inching down towards her slim waist and then over the flare of her hips and onto the contours of her buttocks.

Then I pulled away, dropping the sponge, trying to break free from her hypnotic body. But Carole twisted around to face me, and I stared at her breasts, her nipples, her crotch, and I became immobile once more.

She smiled at me, then reached for the tap and turned the water on. The spray gushed out, rinsing the soap from her body, splashing onto me and wetting my pyjamas.

'Why don't you take your things off?' Carole suggested.

I didn't reply, didn't move – couldn't reply, couldn't move. And I watched as Carole's wet hands reached out towards me, her fingers finding the buttons of my cotton pyjama top and unfastening them, then slipping the garment off my shoulders so that it fell to the floor.

Carole's eyes were on my breasts, and then they dropped lower. I found my thumbs hooking into the elastic of my pants, tugging them down over my hips, letting them drop away, and I stook naked in front of her. The girl surveyed my body, and slowly she smiled.

'That's better, isn't it?' she said. 'Now we've got nothing to hide from each other, have we?' She tilted back her head, letting the water spray onto her face and course down the valley between her ripe breasts. 'Why don't you get into the shower? It's lovely.' She stepped back a pace. 'There's plenty of room.'

Carole had been enjoying herself in the water, so why shouldn't I? It wasn't going to make any difference now what I did, because Carole had already seen me without my clothes. So I stepped over the edge, climbing in next to her, and she moved aside so that I could take the full force of the spray.

'Shall I do your back?' she asked, bending to pick up the sponge, her buttocks brushing against my legs.

I turned my back in silent acceptance. I was thoroughly soaked by now, and Carole switched off the shower and began to stroke the soapy sponge across my shoulder blades. And she was right, it was a wonderful sensation, and I closed my eyes as I enjoyed the unique luxury of having someone wash me.

I hardly noticed as her hands slipped beneath my arms, still softly rubbing, and worked their way towards my breasts, cupping them in her palms and gently stroking them, caressing my firm nipples between her fingers. This felt even better, and my breath came in shorter and shorter gasps.

Then her right hand slid away from my right breast, gliding down across my ribs and over my waist, brushing lightly across my pubic hairs. That was when I opened my eyes, watching as one of Carole's fingers hesitantly probed into the top of my cleft. I twisted around quickly, and both of her hands fell away.

We were face to face, our breasts pressed against each other's. Carole's hands went around my waist, then dropped a few inches to rest on my buttocks. I gripped her wrists, and our eyes met. I let go, then tentatively I reached out to touch her, my right hand reaching for her shoulder, while my left touched her hip, feeling the hardness of bone beneath the supple flesh.

Slowly Carole's face moved towards mine, as her tongue darted out to moisten her upper lip.

We kissed.

My first kiss.

Our lips lightly brushed against each other's, then pushed more forcefully until they were pressed hard together. Carole's mouth opened, and I felt her tongue lightly stroke the line between my lips. Then she

32

pushed harder, trying to probe inside but meeting only my firmly clamped teeth. I tried to pull back, but now one of Carole's hands was at the back of my head, holding me rigid, while her tongue kept probing.

I allowed my mouth to open slightly, and then Carole's tongue eased its way inside, finding my own tongue and pushing against it. This was so unexpected, and I thrust my tongue at hers, trying to force it away. But instead her tongue entwined with mine, gently stroking it. Carole's eyes were shut, her face slowly turning from side to side as she rubbed her lips across mine. We were breathing the same air, and even our hearts seemed to beat in unison.

My tongue began to react, imitating Carole's actions, exploring her tongue, thrusting its way into the sweetness of her mouth, while her teeth gently nipped and her lips sucked at it.

Then I came to my senses and realized what I was doing. I pulled away guiltily, but Carole's hands were still around me and I couldn't retreat far.

Dreamily, she opened her eyes and stared at me, smiling softly. 'What's the matter?'

I shook my head uncertainly, not knowing the answer. This was all wrong. We oughtn't be doing this. Yet it was so pleasurable, so why shouldn't we? I felt confused and bewildered.

Carole was still smiling, and gradually I also smiled. Then I laughed briefly, the laughter dissolving into a fit of giggles. Carole began to giggle, too, and we held each other tight, squeezing our wet bodies together. I felt Carole's crotch against mine, and she started to gyrate her hips, pressing even harder against me. And it was just like when I used to rub myself against the leather saddle when I was riding.

I began to do the same, grinding my mound against the other girl's, our damp pubic hair intertwining. We kissed again, and this time there was no pulling away. Our lips met, our teeth clashing and our tongues fencing as we kissed with frenzied passion, while our

33

hands were everywhere – sliding across one another's pink wet flesh, touching breasts and nipples, thighs and hips and legs . . .

My pulse raced, my breath coming in short gasps, and my whole body seemed to be floating in mid-air. A strange and beautiful sensation was building up within me, and I didn't know what it was because I'd never experienced it before. A kind of warmth which was increasing, increasing, increasing – raising me higher and higher and higher. Promising to take me to a fabulous place where I'd never been and which I could only barely guess at. And if the journey was so wonderful, then how magical would be the ultimate destination?

But before I could arrive, suddenly Carole pulled away. She was panting and gasping as she let go of me, her mouth hanging wide open. She took a step backwards, her left hand going to her right breast, her fingers pinching and twisting at the swollen nipple so hard that it must have hurt. Her right hand dropped to her crotch, the palm covering her pubic hairs, the fingers sliding between her legs. As I watched, I noticed her index and middle finger vanish as she pushed them up inside her vagina. The fingers slid rapidly in and out, as Carole sank onto her knees, her eyes still shut, her mouth wide and a low animal growl escaped from the back of her throat. Her whole body trembled and convulsed as she groaned in ecstasy.

Slowly, she became silent and still, and she opened her eyes and looked up at me.

'I had to do that,' she said breathlessly, letting go of her nipple, 'or I'd have burst.' She pulled her fingers out from within. 'What about you?'

I shrugged. I was feeling vaguely disappointed, having scaled almost to the top of the mountain but not reached the peak.

'Don't you want to bring yourself off?'

I said nothing, because I didn't understand quite what she meant. But unconsciously my hand was

34

fingering my own crotch, finding it damp; but not moist from the shower, rather a kind of slick wetness. I'd seldom touched myself there with my bare hand, and somehow it felt different – more sensitive and with folds and creases I'd never been aware of previously.

Carole must have realized from my expression that I didn't understand what she meant, because she said: 'Don't you ever masturbate?'

I shook my head briefly. I'd never even heard the word before.

Carole stood up again at last. 'You ought to,' she told me. 'It's really great.' She stared at the ceiling, as if searching for the right words. 'It's really great,' she repeated. 'I can't explain the sensation. You've got to try it for yourself.'

Quickly, I pulled my hand away from my crotch, and Carole laughed.

'You aren't shy, are you?' she asked.

I began to chuckle. 'Not any more,' I replied. 'What was that word?'

'Masturbation. To masturbate.' Carole paused, then smiled and added a parody of a language lesson: 'I masturbate; you masturbate; he, she or it masturbates . . .'

'And that was what you were doing now?' I asked. 'With your fingers?'

Carole nodded. 'It's having sex with yourself – who needs some boy's thing when you've got these?' She wriggled her two fingers, thrusting out her tongue from the side of her mouth and widening her eyes in an indecent leer.

I laughed at her imitation of a sex maniac, then Carole reached for the tap and turned the shower on again.

'Come on,' she said. 'Let's get all this soap off us.' She pulled the shower head from its bracket and aimed it at me, rinsing the suds off my body. 'You look really great, you know. Your breasts are so round and firm, and the nipples so pert and pretty. And you're lucky to have blonde hair – it's almost as though you don't have any pubic hair at all, it's so fine it's almost transparent. I wish mine was like yours.'

I turned my back, letting the water gush over my shoulders and down my buttocks and legs.

'Shall I do you?' I suggested, once Carole had finished rinsing me off.

She raised her eyebrows and pursed her lips. 'I'd love you to do me,' she said, smiling. But she didn't give me the shower, instead spraying herself while her other hand slid across her breasts, following the spurt of the water.

'It was in the shower that I had my first orgasm,' she added. 'I was douching myself like this.' She was spraying her crotch now, while her free hand rubbed at her pubis. 'Douching is a fancy name for shooting water up your cunt. You must have done this.' She aimed the spray upwards, spreading her legs, and I saw the pinkness of her most secret place.

'Er . . . sort of,' I said, and I glanced away. It was crazy after what had just occurred, but the sight of her open vagina was more embarrassing than anything else I'd seen or allowed to happen.

Carole noticed that I'd looked away. 'What's wrong?'

I rubbed at my left eye. 'Soap in my eye,' I lied, and I stepped out of the shower and went to the mirror above the basin, wiping the condensation away with the heel of my hand, pretending to examine the reflection of my eye.

'I was simply doing this, thinking how nice it was,' Carole continued. 'Rubbing with just my fingers because I didn't want to get any soap inside me. And the more I rubbed the more I enjoyed it. My lips began to swell, and I found my clitoris for the first time, a tiny fleshy button – but that also began to swell up the more I touched it. Then suddenly – wow! My first proper orgasm. And I've never looked back since.' She sighed nostalgically, her fingers and the fine jets of water continuing to work on her cunt.

I dried myself, then dusted my body with talc before putting on my pyjamas again. Carole was still amusing herself when I left the bathroom.

When she returned to the bedroom a few minutes later, all she was wearing was a towel. It was wrapped around her head like a turban. She sat down on the spare bed next to me, and without a word she took the comb from my hand and continued running it through my damp locks. It sent shivers up and down my spine, a lovely feeling.

'Is something wrong?' Carole asked after about a minute.

'No,' I answered, turning to look at her. 'Such as what?'

She shrugged, her breasts swaying. 'You seemed to leave the bathroom very abruptly.'

'No, I didn't. I'd finished in there, that was all.'

'But you didn't finish, did you? You didn't have a climax. I feel so selfish.' She rested her head on my shoulder for a moment.

'Don't be. It was fine,' I assured her. 'I enjoyed myself, and I don't regret it at all.'

'That's good,' Carole nodded, her eyes sparkling with mischief. 'Because we've only just begun . . .' She tugged the towel off her head, shaking her damp hair and spraying me with fine droplets of water. She stood up, hands on hips and gazed at me. 'Have you ever had an orgasm?'

I wasn't sure. I didn't think so. I'd certainly never experienced such an internal earthquake as had seemed to shake Carole a while ago.

'Well?' Carole prompted, like a school teacher waiting for the answer to a question she'd set.

I shrugged.

'Then tonight's the night,' she assured me.

I opened my mouth, but then closed it again because I wasn't certain what I wanted to say. This all seemed too organized, like a task I was being set or a lesson I was forced to learn. I'd already decided that I was going to masturbate tonight, to give myself an orgasm, determined to succeed even if it took me until dawn. But I wanted to do it by myself, I didn't need Carole – she'd pointed out the route, and I could find my own way there.

Carole was standing naked in front of me, and now her hands slid from her hips towards her crotch. 'Look,' she said, and her fingertips pulled open her fleshy outer cunt lips.

Immediately I turned my head. This should be Carole's alone, shared with no one.

'What's wrong?' she asked in bewilderment. 'You've got to know what you're doing.' But when my eyes remained focused away, she shook her head in exasperation. 'Okay, take your pyjamas off. Don't be shy.' She laughed, turning and going towards the dressing table in the far corner of the room.

I undid the buttons and shrugged off my jacket, then I pulled down the lower half of my pyjamas. Carole came back, holding a large mirror with a round wooden handle. She passed it to me.

'Say hello to your cunt,' she told me. 'You've never looked before, have you? So open your legs and introduce yourself. Make friends, you'll have hours of endless fun together . . .' Then she turned away and left the room, letting me know that what I did was up to me.

I raised the mirror, studying my face, staring deep into my own eyes as though they were those of a stranger. Then I moved the mirror down, examining both of my breasts and the dimpled erect nipples. I still felt a kind of aching void in my loins. It was a bit like being hungry and all set to eat a meal, smelling its delicious odours and almost tasting the flavours and texture, but then discovering there was no food left.

I was sitting on the edge of the spare bed, and hesitantly I let the mirror descend even further, and I opened my legs. There was too much shadow to see any detail. All I could make out were soft wisps of blonde hair and vague pink outlines. I sat further back on the bed, resting my heels on the edge and widening my knees as far as they would go, and I leaned forward to peer into the mirror, my free hand gently tracing the contours of what I could see.

After a few seconds I became aware that Carole had returned, and I heard her throw something onto her bed, but I kept my attention on what I was doing, amazed at how new and strange it all was – this had been part of me all my life, but I'd been almost totally unaware of it.

'Those are the lips,' said Carole, also watching. 'There's the inner and outer. The inner ones, yes those, are the sensitive ones. And right in the centre is your pleasure button. There, yes. That's your clitoris. Give it a stroke. Lick your finger first if you want. You can bring yourself off just by rubbing your clit. Or you can stick a finger or two inside your cunt and slide them in and out. Or you can do both. Yeah, you've got it. Push in there, go on.'

But I didn't. I removed both my hand and the mirror.

Carole was still staring at my open crotch, and she rubbed her hand across her pubis. She exhaled noisily between her teeth.

'You're giving me the hots again,' she said, and she sat down on the bed by my side, draping her arms around my shoulders. 'Give me a kiss.'

Our lips touched, rubbing and nuzzling, chewing lightly at each other, teasing the soft flesh, nibbling and sucking. After a few seconds, our mouths opened and our tongues met.

I felt one of Carole's hands on my breast, while the other slipped down my side and over my stomach; but I shut my legs firmly before it reached its target, and she stroked the top of my thighs instead. Her lips pulled away from mine, and she bent her head, taking my right nipple in her mouth and gently sucking, her teeth lightly raking the delicate pink flesh, her tongue caressing it to even greater dimensions. And it was marvellous.

It seemed obvious what Carole wished me to do, that she wanted my fingers to find her cunt, to explore the warm damp folds, to tease her clitoris and plunge deep inside her. But I couldn't bring myself to do that, and instead I drew back so that her lips released my nipple, and I leaned down to take one of her breasts to my own mouth.

'Ahhhhh,' she sighed, as my tongue circled the nipple, my lips sucking as though it was an exquisite succulent ripe fruit, and to me it tasted even better.

Carole ran her fingers through my hair, then caressed my breasts. 'Shall we go over to my bed? There's more space.'

We crossed the room and sat on the other bed, resuming kissing, then after a few seconds we tumbled backwards and lay together, embracing one another.

After a minute, Carole reluctantly pulled her mouth free from mine. 'I've got to do it again,' she said. 'I know you don't want to do it to me, but I've got to have a finger fuck.' She paused. 'Or maybe I can use something else. Almost anything will do. I've even used the handle of that mirror over there.' As she spoke, the heel of her hand was grinding against the bony mound beneath her dark pubic hairs.

And I too could feel the tension building up within me, the pressure increasing all the time.

'You know they even make special things for women to fuck themselves?' Carole continued. 'Dildoes, they're called. And there are battery-powered ones called vibrators.'

I laughed, while my right hand tentatively reached between my legs.

'It's true,' Carole stated. 'Don't you believe me? I'd love to try one. They come in all shapes and sizes and designs. You use them against your clit or shove them right up inside. Saves wearing out your fingers, I suppose.' It was her turn to laugh. 'They even have ones which shoot warm liquid up you, just like a boy's spurting thing. But I like bananas,' she added suddenly.

I stroked my clitoris lightly, which sent a shiver of pleasure from my toes to my head. 'What?' I asked, wondering what she was talking about.

Carole sat up. 'Here,' she said, reaching for what she'd thrown onto the bed earlier. Two bananas, green and unripe. She leaned against the wall, drawing up her knees, and for the first time I saw her cunt in detail; and I didn't look away. My finger followed the folds of my own twat as I watched hers.

'Want one?' Carole asked, splitting the bananas from each other and holding one out to me.

'Not just at the moment,' I said, mystified.

She put one down and started to unpeel the other. 'The shape's just right, they could have been specially designed for the purpose. You can use it with the skin on, but I prefer it peeled. Not a ripe one, because it'll dissolve and go all messy. A good firm one like this, all nice and slimy on the outside.' She threw the skin onto the floor, stroking the length of the fruit as she spoke.

She looked at me briefly. I was still lying stretched out on the bed, my head on a level with her drawn up and spread legs.

Carole reached down with her left hand, thumb and forefinger opening her inner labia. Then her other hand came down with the banana, gently pushing the rounded end against her cunt. I watched in amazement. Surely the thing was too wide. But slowly, surely, she inserted it deeper and deeper until half its length had disappeared inside her.

Her eyes were closed, and she sighed luxuriously. She twisted the banana a few degrees one way, then back in the other direction, and she groaned with pleasure. After a few turns, she started to slide the fruit a small way in and out, and I could see it rub against her labia and clitoris. She moaned even louder now.

I raised myself on one elbow and picked up the second banana, swiftly peeling off the skin. It seemed

41

too big. I'd never get it inside me. Yet Carole had managed somehow, and she was so evidently enjoying the experience that I just had to give it a try or else I'd never know what it was like. It was now or never.

I sat up, drawing up my legs and facing Carole, our knees touching. Her eyes opened at this contact, and she watched as I repeated what she'd done. I rubbed the tip of the banana against the edge of my cunt, stroking my clit, gently finding an opening between my moist lips. The first touch was wonderful, and I shuddered with enjoyment.

Carole reached forward, and I felt her fingers brush against my twat as she guided the fruit into my opening. I groaned, shutting my eyes in sybaritic joy, my fingers dropping away as I let Carole take over and ease the banana into my cunt, twisting it so that it stroked the walls of my vagina, pulling it back a fraction to rub gently against my swollen clit, then shoving it even deeper.

I moved closer to her, so that we sat between each other's legs. Carole had a banana in each hand, moving them in parallel so that we felt the same almost unbearable sensation simultaneously. I leaned back, taking my weight on my hands. Carole was doing all the work, but I couldn't have moved a muscle at that time, my whole body was lost as it climbed towards the ultimate pleasure.

Then the delicious movement between my legs stopped, and I opened my eyes. Carole was holding half a banana in her hand, the one within me had snapped. She looked at me, and we both giggled. I reached forward with one hand to pull the broken fruit out, but Carole prevented me from retrieving it, pushing me down to my previous position.

Weakly, I fell back, watching as Carole bent over me. Her head descended towards my crotch. I felt her hot breath, her warm lips and her wet tongue as her teeth seized the end of the banana. She began to eat the fruit, drawing it from me fractionally with every bite, while her tongue licked against the warm tongue of my clitoris and her lips nuzzled the tender lips of my twat.

It was the most exquisite sensation I'd ever experienced.

There was no way that I could have absorbed so much sheer delight, I had to let Carole share this.

I tried to pull away, but she put her hands around my hips to restrain me, misunderstanding my motives. I stroked the crown of her head, dropping my hands down the side of her face to her mouth, feeling her lips against my cunt, and gently I pushed her away while I slid backwards.

Carole tugged the last of the banana free and swallowed it. I moved around on my right side, bringing my own head between her legs, reaching out to draw her towards me.

She understood, and she also lay down on her right side next to me, her head the other way so that her face was opposite my crotch while mine was by hers. I raised my left leg, bending it at the knee, and Carole did the same. She pulled the remains of her own banana free, casting it aside.

And we kissed each other's cunts.

My tongue probed and caressed the soft sweetness which was at the heart of Carole's womanhood, my lips sucking at the moist flesh – while her devouring mouth was rapidly bringing me towards the absolute peak.

The sensation was beyond all imagining. And as my whole body exploded with the ultimate experience, my tongue and lips felt the first shuddering ripples within Carole's cunt as she too began to climax. Our hands and fingers clawed at one another in helpless abandon.

I shook and trembled, moaned and cried out, every sense more aware than ever before as I experienced my first shattering orgasm, my whole being exceeding the boundless limits of ecstasy.

43

Chapter Four

When I woke up the next morning, I was in bed with Carole, our limbs intertwined. It was so nice simply to lie there in her arms, watching her sleeping face. I'd never felt so content in my life. At last her eyes twitched as she floated towards consciousness, and then she blinked and was awake.

'Hello,' she said, smiling, as she hugged me close against her nude body.

'Hello,' I echoed, kissing her lightly on the lips.

'That was a wonderful night, wasn't it?'

'What night?' I asked.

Carole frowned, puzzled. Then she laughed and tugged playfully at my pubic hairs. 'For a moment I thought I'd been dreaming,' she told me.

'It was great,' I agreed at last. 'Thanks for inviting me around. Did you have my seduction all planned out?'

She shook her head. 'How could I have planned that? But I did have my hopes – although I never imagined it could have worked out so well.' She smiled as she remembered.

'Have you ever done that before?' I asked.

'Done what? I've done everything a girl can do by herself, or I think I have. But with two of us, it's far more than twice as good.'

'Then you haven't been to bed with another girl?'

Carole looked surprised. She shook her head. 'No of course not – you're the first. What I really wanted to discover was what it's like to have my cunt licked. That's about the only thing I can't manage on my own! And I bet a girl can perform cunnilingus better than any man.'

'Cunny what?'

'Cunnilingus. It means cunt sucking.'

'You're kidding,' I said. 'There can't be a word for that.' But until a few hours ago I'd never guessed such a thing was ever done or even possible; the idea would have repulsed me. It was such a terrific experience, however, that I could hardly wait to try it again . . .

'Of course there is,' Carole assured me. 'There's a word for everything – and we're both lesbians now, aren't we?'

That was a word I had heard of. 'Lesbian,' I repeated, rolling the sound around my mouth. The idea of sex without men had always seemed very attractive, sort of clean and wholesome. And as Carole had implied, who knew a girl's sexual preferences better than another girl?

'How about some breakfast?' Carole asked, stretching out her arms, the bed covers falling off to expose the roundness of her breasts.

'Breakfast in bed?' I said, raising my eyebrows.

'Good idea,' she nodded thoughtfully. Our eyes met. 'And I know exactly what I'd like to eat . . .'

That Sunday morning, for the first time in ages, neither of us went horse riding.

Carole and I were the closest of friends for two years. We went everywhere together, did everything together. We even went on holiday a couple of times, sharing the same room, the same bed – and of course each other's bodies. But when Carole left school and took a job, it was inevitable that we would drift apart. Our passion was no longer so intense, the flames dying down over the months.

And then Carole found another lover – his name was Peter. I don't know whether it was worse her going off with a man rather than another girl, but it took me a long time to get over her treachery. One day we were sharing a double-headed vibrator, and the next she was in bed with this guy Peter.

Then it was my turn to leave school and find a job. I began working in one of the offices of the largest factory in town. There were five other girls there, all of them within a few years of my own age. The office was run by a fifty-year-old sexless tyrant, and you could only tell she was a woman because of her name, Miss Tresson.

Because I was the office junior, I was given the most boring and menial tasks to do. But I got on quite well with the other five, and a few of us would go out for lunch once a week as a change from the canteen. Sometimes we might even get together for a drink in the evening, although this was rare because the others all had boyfriends – either steadies or a whole sequence of brief affairs.

I was very lonely. It's easy for girls to pick up men, but to find other girls is so much more difficult. A couple of the girls from the office were always trying to fix me up with dates, because they thought I was too shy to find myself a boyfriend. But there was no way that I could tell them what it was I really needed. To make it worse, I fell in love with one of the girls.

Her name was Sue, a petite redhead of twenty. She was the kind of person who reaches out to touch or put her arm around you when she's talking. But she did this to all the other girls in the office, in a friendly girlish way – not in any sexual fashion.

Sue had a number of boyfriends, and she'd often confide in me about the trouble they gave her, the things she had to put up with. But she never learned. There'd always be another man in her life to treat her as badly as the others. Yet she could have had me. I loved her far more than any male ever would, could do things for her that she'd never imagined possible. I'd lie awake in my lonely bed, masturbating, and wishing that Sue was there with me; then I'd dream an erotic fantasy about her, and that would leave me even more frustrated.

The next day I'd see her again, watching her mouth as she talked to me and wishing I could taste those soft red lips and that delicious pink tongue, trying not to gaze too long at the rise of her upturned breasts, imagining what she looked like in the nude, unable to ignore the image of myself gazing down and watching Sue's cropped red hair between my legs as her tongue thrust deep into my aching cunt.

Twice I even went out on dates with Sue, to keep her company when she'd arranged to meet some guy and his friend. Both times I hoped that it would be she and I who paired off, but it didn't work out like that. What happened was that I'd be stuck with some ape who thought that for the price of a couple of drinks he was entitled to shove his prick into me, or at the very least stuff his fat tongue down my throat. Each time I managed to get away safe, but the story got back to Sue – and I could never forgive her for the callous way that she passed it on to the others in the office. She didn't mean any harm by it, I know. The rest of them treated it as a joke, thinking that I must be very innocent and scared of men. The latter might have been true, but the first certainly wasn't.

The girls had arranged to go to a nightclub called The Oasis, and they invited me to join them.

'I know we've been rotten to you lately,' Sue said one lunchtime, 'teasing you about those boys you met. So why don't you come along? It should be a laugh. It's a girls-only night.'

That was what clinched it. Girls only. I'd never been to The Oasis before, although I'd heard about it; it was meant to be quite a place.

'Okay,' I agreed, thinking what a good time I'd had when I'd been out in the evenings with the office gang. I didn't know what was meant by a girls-only night, but it sounded promising. Maybe I could meet up with another girl who shared my own personal sexual preference.

'That's good,' Sue told me, 'because we've already got you this.' She opened her bag and handed me the ticket. It was dated for the following Friday. Then I saw the price.

47

'You had to pay for it?' I asked.

'That's right. It's to cover the hire of the room, pay for the entertainment and for food. Drinks come extra – you drink as much as you can pay for.' Sue smiled at me, and I tried not to stare at her perfect lips.

'It sounds quite elaborate,' I said, reaching for my purse and opening it. 'What kind of entertainment?' I counted out the money and offered it to her.

But Sue shook her head. 'No, no, no,' she said. 'The rest of us paid for you. We always go every year, and it's a tradition that the junior doesn't have to pay – because of what she has to put up with the rest of the time here.'

'Are you sure?' I didn't want any special favours.

'Sure I'm sure. When I started here two years ago, the others paid for me.' She stared absently up at the ceiling for a moment, as though reminiscing, and she half smiled. 'It's a chance for all the girls who work here – in the offices or on the shop floor – to let our hair down away from husbands and boyfriends.'

'Does Miss Tresson go?' I asked, wondering if it was possible for our supervisor to let her hair down.

Sue laughed out loud and shook her head. 'No,' she promised, 'she certainly doesn't.'

So the next Friday, I put on my best clothes – a pair of tight black satin pants, a bright red cotton blouse and jet black velvet waistcoat, as well as a pair of red leather ankle boots – donned my woollen coat and went off to rendezvous with Sue.

We went in through the entrance of The Oasis, showing our tickets to the bouncer at the door, and he directed us up a flight of stairs to a room on the top floor. There must have been about two hundred women in there, sitting at the tables which lined two opposite walls, or standing by the bar which ran the full length of the wall by the entrance. There was a stage against the far wall, and a disc jockey was up there playing records. She was female – as was the staff behind the bar.

The lights were turned low, a rainbow sequence of coloured spotlights spinning from a complex array in the centre of the ceiling, flashing in rhythm to the pounding disco beat. Several girls were dancing, and I glanced at them. Sue and I found the other four from our office – Jean and Trisha, Lynne and Rose – and I bought them all a drink because they'd paid for my ticket. The drinks came to more than the price of my ticket, but the money didn't matter. As soon as I'd stepped through the door, I knew I was going to enjoy myself; and after a couple of drinks I was convinced of it. Two hundred girls – I was bound to find one who shared my unusual tastes.

The other four had taken over one of the round tables on the left-hand side of the room, about halfway towards the low stage, and we talked about all kinds of things. We had to raise our voices to make ourselves heard above the music, and the only taboo subject was work.

I was watching the dancers, my fingers tapping the table top, and Sue must have noticed because she said: 'Shall we go and dance?'

I stared at her, trying not to show my eagerness, and I shrugged. 'Could do,' I said casually, rising to my feet.

We walked towards the centre of the room, and I was a couple of paces behind Sue, watching the sway of her hips. She was snapping her fingers, her shoulders rocking from side to side with the beat. Then she stopped, half turned towards me, and she started dancing. I stayed a few feet from her as my body also began to move, watching her all the time. But Sue wasn't looking at me, only through me. I knew she'd come out here in response to the music – that she simply wanted to dance, it had nothing to do with me – but I couldn't accept that on an emotional level.

I longed for a slow number to be played, so that I could hold the slim redhead in my arms and pull her close against me, letting my touch demonstrate what I felt for her; but there was little chance of that.

I stared at the way she moved, at her arms and legs flowing with the rhythm, at her breasts gently bouncing up and down, and I thought of how she would look when her body was twisting and writhing in the ecstasy of lovemaking. And I knew it was futile, that she would never be mine.

So I began to focus my attention elsewhere, searching for a pair of eyes which would meet and hold my own. I must have been quite a distinctive figure with my flowing blonde hair, my breasts jiggling unfettered beneath my blouse. But whenever I noticed another girl watching me and I turned my head, she would glance away.

After a few minutes, the music faded away, the flashing coloured lights ceased to revolve, and some of the main lighting came on again. 'If you want to take your places, girls,' said the deejay over the bank of speakers next to the record console, 'the evening's entertainment will be commencing shortly.'

There was a cheer and some scattered applause from the audience. Sue and I went to the bar for another drink, and we stopped at the buffet table to fill a couple of plates before we returned to our places. My seat was on the outside of the table, my back to the stage; but if I turned my chair I'd be able to see what was going on. For the moment, I was content to eat and drink.

'Thank you, girls,' called the announcer. 'I'd like you to give a warm welcome to – Sammy!'

The cheering and applause was even louder this time, and there were even a few piercing whistles from the crowd. I turned my head, wondering what was going on.

A man appeared on the stage. He was about six foot high, around twenty-five years old and wearing evening dress. Some kind of singer, I guessed.

Then I heard someone shout: 'Look at his balls!'

The remark brought hoots of laughter and loud jeers,

and I took a closer look at the man. In one hand he was carrying two balls, the size of tennis balls, and in the other he held a club. A juggler? I could hardly believe it. Was this the kind of entertainment everyone seemed to be awaiting so eagerly?

Sammy took a deep bow, and when he stood up he was holding the two balls and the club against his crotch. Slowly he raised the club towards the vertical in a bizarre imitation of an erect phallus, and he was rewarded with gales of cheers and laughter. This was really subtle stuff. I glanced at Sue, and she shrugged disparagingly. I smiled briefly, and she mirrored my expression.

The guy started juggling with the balls and club, while in the background a tape of soft rock music played. He held my interest for about two seconds, then I turned away and studied the audience, amazed by how fascinated they seemed to be in what he was doing. When next I turned around, prompted by a cheer, he had removed his jacket and was ripping off his shirt, tearing away the buttons like Clark Kent about to reveal his secret identity as Superman. But what he did reveal was a broad naked chest, totally hairless, although he still wore his bow tie around his bare neck.

The juggler had been transformed into a fire eater. He'd stepped down from the stage to the middle of the room, and the lights were dimmed as he stroked his arms and chest with burning brands, quenching the flames by thrusting them into his mouth. He strode towards a table on the other side of the room, holding the final flaming rod ahead of him like an Olympic runner, and all those sitting there squealed and leaned away – while everyone else roared with laughter.

He kicked his shoes off, running the flickering flames across his bare feet, then thrust the blazing torch into his mouth, exhaling a bright inferno of fire, and there wasn't even a spark left. Cheers and applause followed, and even I clapped my hands in appreciation.

Then he dropped his trousers and stood in the centre of the room clad only in a pair of tight leather shorts which were held together by a criss-cross of laces on each hip. There were more cheers and laughter, and the music picked up tempo and volume as he started to dance. He danced across the floor, from table to table, rotating his buttocks and thrusting out his groin. Though I was astounded by some of what he did, I had to admit he was a great athlete. His body was trim, the muscles well toned, and without any apparent effort he could turn cartwheels and somersaults as he flaunted himself at every table. Almost everywhere, hands reached out to stroke his arms or legs, tugging at the ends of the laces in an attempt to tear away his leather shorts.

And finally I realized why they'd all been paying him so much attention earlier – Sammy was a male stripper!

How far was he going to go? Female strippers took off everything, I knew, so did that mean he would too? I stared at the other five seated around my table, at their eager expressions, and I realized that he must strip right off or else they wouldn't be getting so excited.

One row of laces had almost been ripped away, and his shorts were hanging half off as he came to our table. Rose reached out and tweaked one of his nipples, while Jean slapped his almost bare buttock and began tugging at the other laces.

Sammy was standing right next to me when his shorts fell away, but he was still wearing a kind of G-string, a brief cotton pouch which did its best to cover his genitals; and he still had on his incongruous bow tie. I turned away, dimly aware of the uproar which had broken out at the almost total revelation. But Sammy stayed by my side, rocking his hips to and fro at me, slipping his hand inside his tiny garment.

I picked up my drink and began sipping at it, trying to turn my chair away, but he was holding it down with one of his feet and I couldn't get away from him. Then suddenly Sue reached across and grabbed at the side of the G-string, yanking it away – and the man's naked cock and balls were a few inches from my face! I stared in terrified fascination, unable to close my eyes or look away.

I could hardly believe it. Of all the other women in the room, why did he have to choose me?

His was the first adult prick I'd ever seen. It was much longer and fatter than I had imagined. And I thought it looked so ugly and clumsy, not at all beautiful like Carole's cunt, but like some strange creature hanging out from its nest of dark hairs. Yet there was something hypnotically attractive about its latent power and raw animal aggressiveness.

My glass was still held defensively against my mouth, but Sammy reached for it and pulled it from my fingers. I watched in horror as he dipped his tool into my drink, stirring it as though it was some huge cocktail stick, and I noticed the other girls near me laughing out loud. Then the man pulled out his prick, and thrust it towards my mouth, spraying alcohol from the end of his knob onto my face. I jerked my head back, but I was still unable to leave my chair; it was as though I'd been tied to it like a torture victim.

The man grinned at me, stroking the length of his big pink shaft, and I saw the thing begin to stir of its own accord. He was getting an erection. I was frozen, wondering what he intended to do next. Was he going to carry out oral rape in public, forcing his penis between my lips in front of all these people? It seemed entirely possible, because no one else seemed to care. The whole room was erupted into a cacophony of cheering and laughter, urging him on.

Letting go of his half stiff member, he jerked his hips up and down at me, reaching for and unfastening his bow tie, bringing it down and swiftly tying it around the middle of his tool, as though it was some ribboned gift. He stepped closer, his penis now horizontal and aimed directly at my mouth.

Distantly, I could hear a synchronized clapping and Sammy was thrusting his cock in time to the audience's enthusiastic beats of applause. Everyone was clapping, even Sue. The swollen purple glans inched its way nearer to me. I started to cry. I hadn't cried for years, but unbidden the tears welled up in my eyes, spilled over and dripped down my cheeks.

It was crazy, but I couldn't help it. Then I reached for my glass where Sammy had replaced it on the table, picked it up and poured my drink all over his offensive weapon. He sprang aside, but I saw he was still grinning as he backed towards the next table. I stood up and without hurry walked away, staring at the floor and hoping no one would see my stupid tears.

'Wait!' I heard a voice behind me, recognizing it as Sue's, and I changed my direction slightly. 'Don't go,' the girl begged, catching up with me and putting her hand on my arm.

'Go?' I said as I reached the bar. 'Who's going anywhere? I just want another drink. You didn't really expect me to finish off that glass after he'd washed his dick in it, did you?'

Sue half smiled, but she must have observed my tears and known that I had been about to leave. 'I'll get these,' she said, as I ordered my drink. 'I could do with another one, too.'

We stood at the bar. Sammy was still busy performing for his appreciative audience. He was standing on one of the tables now, while a tall brunette was trying to unfasten his bow tie with her teeth, hampered by the fact that he kept swinging his cock into her face.

'I'm sorry,' said Sue. 'I didn't think it would be like that.'

I shrugged. 'It's not your fault,' I assured her. 'I didn't have to come here.'

Sue didn't reply, and I noticed her concerned expression – and I realized it was her fault. This had all been

54

arranged. It wasn't chance that Sammy had picked me out.

The girl noticed me watching her. 'It was just meant to be a bit of fun,' she explained. 'It happened to me a couple of years ago, when I was new here as well. But it was nothing like this, the way that bastard went for you. I was embarrassed by him suddenly coming up behind me and poking his cock over my shoulder, but not totally humiliated. No, what that guy did just wasn't fair, particularly with you being . . . well . . . you know.' She shook her head, watching as Sammy danced nude in the centre of the floor, his prick flopping up and down, beating against his stomach and thighs.

'What am I?' I asked, puzzled.

'You know,' Sue answered, glancing around. Then she lowered her voice as though about to utter the most foul obscenity ever deleted from a dictionary. 'A virgin.'

Her remark threw me a moment. I'd never considered myself a virgin, not after my long affair with Carole, but I supposed that I was.

The others had arranged for Sammy to chose me from the audience, but he'd gone further than they'd expected. And the reason they'd done it was because they thought I was sexually innocent. When it came to men, I was; but that was only a part of the story.

Yet there was no harm done. The whole incident had only lasted a couple of minutes, and it was kind of funny in a way – or it was now it was over.

'At least he didn't come all over me,' I remarked casually, 'particularly since I've just washed my hair.'

Sue stared at me in amazement, and I laughed aloud. The girl smiled and put her arm around my shoulder, hugging me close. She kissed me lightly on the cheek, and I felt the warmth of her breasts against my body. I turned my head swiftly, and her lips briefly brushed against mine. Sue pulled away, her fingers going uncertainly to her lips.

55

And I knew that was as close as I would ever get to her.

'Does he come?' I asked, nodding towards Sammy, now walking on his hands.

'I doubt it,' Sue said. 'Sex discrimination, isn't it? Wide open cunts in sex magazines for men, but we're not allowed to see erections. And what good is a dangling cock to anyone?' She glanced at me. 'Why do you ask?'

I shrugged.

'He's versatile,' Sue commented, when I didn't reply. 'I wonder if he'll do an imitation of a hat-stand?'

'What's that?' I wanted to know.

'Hanging a hat over the end of his hard-on. One of my old boyfriends used to think it highly amusing.'

'Was it?'

'At least it covered up his cock!'

We both laughed.

Then Sue's face became serious again, and she took a gulp from her drink. 'I think we ought to do something with that Sammy for taking such liberties with you.' She nodded her head slowly, watching as the man vanished behind the curtains to thunderous applause and cheers and whistles. 'I'll go and see the others, find out what they say.'

Ten minutes later, Sue and I had found our way to Sammy's dressing room. I knocked on the door. A moment later it opened and the man peered out. He frowned, then recognized me.

'Hello there,' he said. 'What can I do for you?'

'It's more what I can do for you,' I told him, grinning.

'What we can do for you,' Sue corrected.

Sammy noticed her for the first time, and he stepped back. 'Come in, come in,' he said. 'It's always nice to meet my fans.' He was wearing a knee-length dressing gown, and he shut the door behind us. It was a small room, with a couch and a single chair the only furniture. He glanced at us expectantly.

'We enjoyed your performance,' said Sue.

'That's right,' I added. 'I'd have liked to respond a bit more to what you were doing earlier, but I'm very shy in public. Maybe I can make up for it now?'

Sammy licked at his lips, glancing at us both, unable to believe his luck. He didn't seem aware of how much he'd upset me before. Perhaps he thought it was only natural we should arrive backstage; maybe this was what usually happened after he'd finished his act.

'Yeah, you really turned us on,' said Sue. 'My pussy got so hot and wet that I must have a few inches of cock sliding into me or else I'll have to frig myself off. So how about it?'

'Both of you?' he asked.

'From what we've seen,' said Sue, nodding in the direction of his crotch, 'there's plenty for both of us.'

I felt very nervous and was letting her do most of the talking; she was the one who had experience of men. Sue was handling it far better than I could – though I was surprised by what she was actually saying to him.

She wore a short green woollen skirt, and she tugged it upwards, flashing her white panties, her hand brushing across her crotch. I saw with delight how prominent was her pubis, noticing a couple of red curls which had escaped from the hem of the tight garment, and my heart began to beat even faster.

'Who do you want first?' Sue asked, letting her skirt fall back to cover herself and reaching for the belt of the man's dressing gown.

He was smiling broadly now, and he let Sue unfasten his belt and pull open his garment. His cock could be seen in the shadows, already beginning to rise.

'How do you manage to keep control out there and not get a hard-on?' Sue wanted to know, pulling the dressing gown off his shoulders.

'Trade secret,' Sammy smiled, his hand going down to stroke the full length of his stiffening prick.

57

Sue pushed him towards the couch. 'We've got a few secrets, too,' she murmured. 'You just lie back and we'll show you what I mean. We were worried that you might have jerked yourself off before the performance and you wouldn't have any spunk left for little old us.'

'Don't worry your pretty little head over that,' Sammy said, as he lay down.

'I'm not worried,' Sue told him, while I opened the door. 'You're the one who ought to do the worrying.'

Lynne and Jean and Rose and Trisha piled into the room, and before Sammy knew what was going on they'd got him pinned down, each seizing an arm or a leg. He tried to struggle, but he couldn't move.

'What's going on?' he demanded, looking worried. He forced a grin. 'One at a time girls, hey? Why don't you form a queue outside, hey?'

'Shut up,' said Sue, and she flicked his dick with her finger.

Sammy shouted out in surprised pain, but as he opened his mouth Sue shoved a wad of tissue inside and he was instantly silent. Then she tied him up, binding his wrists and ankles to the four corners of the couch, and the other girls released their grip. He gazed frantically at us, his eyes wide, his cock wilting.

'You went too far tonight, Sammy,' Sue told him, and she glanced at me. 'What do we do with him?'

The helpless man was shaking his head desperately from side to side. I felt a bit sorry for him, because he was so weak and powerless when a handful of girls lined up against him. Yet these were the very ones who had arranged for him to pick me out of the audience, so they must share the blame.

I'd already thought up something suitable; Sammy needed to find out what it was like to be on the receiving end of sexual harassment. He might even like it, and it was also one way of getting back at the five girls – although I'd seen a poster on the wall of the club which had given me another idea of how I might take my revenge against them.

The other girls were watching me, waiting, and I smiled a wicked smile.

'I want you to masturbate him,' I said, and each of them looked uneasy at the prospect.

I wasn't sure why this should have been so. They must all have done it for their boyfriends, so what was so different about Sammy? The problem was that they'd probably never done such a thing when there were other girls present, and they felt uncomfortable. But it wasn't as if I was asking them to strip and fuck him, or even to suck him off. They only had to use their hands.

They knew they owed me this after the stunt they'd pulled, and so reluctantly they went to work.

Sue started first, her fingertips manipulating Sammy's shrunken organ, and I envied him her attention. But she met with little success, because he was so scared.

'Come on, help me,' she said to the others. 'We've got to work on his whole body.'

So the rest of them joined in, stroking the supine man's legs and thighs, his face and neck, his arms and nipples, and gradually his penis began to rise and become rigid. Sue let go, and Lynne took over, working against his length with the clenched fist of her right hand, caressing his testicles with the fingers of her left. Then it was Jean's turn, and she wet her palm with saliva and concentrated on the tip of Sammy's knob, sliding the foreskin to and fro with short rapid strokes.

I tried to watch disinterestedly, but I could feel my labia becoming moist with sexual excitement. I tried to tell myself this was because of watching the girls in action, but I wasn't convinced. After a while instead of imagining that it was me lying naked on the couch, while the girls tortured me so luxuriously, I began to wonder what it would be like to have Sammy's hardness thrusting into my cunt . . .

Soon after Rose had taken the helm, the lucky penis began to twitch of its own volition. There were only a few spurts, the first of which squirted several creamy drops of semen three or four inches onto the man's chest; then a few more sticky drips oozed from the tip and slowly ran down towards his hips and onto the couch.

And it was over. I wasn't very impressed; I hadn't missed anything after all.

Rose wiped her fingers on Sammy's leg, and Trisha looked relieved that she hadn't been forced to lend such an intimate hand. They and the others made for the door.

I stood by Sammy's side, staring down at him. He was watching me cautiously, wondering what was going to happen to him next. But I simply looked at his deflating organ, all red from the action it had experienced. I noticed the tiny pool of spunk above his navel, the first time I'd seen any – but there had been a lot of firsts today.

The first time I'd seen a penis so closely; the first erection I'd watched; the first male climax I'd witnessed. Tentatively, I reached out my right index finger, dipping it into the drops of semen. The stuff felt warm, and I lifted it to my nose and smelled it; but there was nothing to smell. I rubbed it between my finger and thumb, studying the slimy texture and the way it clung to my skin, then dried and was absorbed into my flesh.

Sammy didn't seen too happy in his post-orgasmic rapture. I shook my head slowly as if in disappointment then backed away and headed for the door.

' 'Bye, Sammy,' I called, turning and blowing him a farewell kiss. 'Nice to have seen you.' I made sure the door was ajar so that someone would find him.

As I went down the steps towards the exit, I took another look at the notice I'd seen earlier.

Chapter Five

'I'd like to see The Oasis again under different circumstances,' I said on Monday morning, when we all were taking our coffee break. 'Why don't we go again this Friday, the six of us. I don't think Sammy will be there.'

'No,' agreed Rose, 'it'll be a long time before he shows his face again.'

'Or anything else!' said Sue, and we all laughed.

'I feel a bit guilty about what happened to him,' I said. 'After all, he'd only been doing his job.'

'Don't feel sorry for him,' Jean told me. 'He loved it – he got more out of it than we did. It'll make a great story for him to tell his friends, how he was stripped and jerked off by six girls.'

'That's right,' Trisha agreed. 'If you pay as much attention to a guy's cock as you do the rest of his body, you can't go wrong.' She was looking at me as she spoke, offering me sisterly advice on how to keep a man.

'Yeah,' nodded Lynne. 'That's why the first thing they try to do is shove a couple of fingers up your honey pot, thinking they're doing you a favour, because there's nothing they like better than a hand on their tool – they're so used to giving themselves a manual, you see.'

I could tell they all felt guilty for what had happened to me on Friday, although I was no longer bothered; yet they couldn't bring themselves to make an explicit apology and so they were doing it in a circuitous way. I'd never heard them talk so frankly about sex before. As I listened, I nodded my head even though I knew that I'd never benefit from their knowledge and experience.

'So what about Friday?' I asked.

'I've got a date,' said Rose.

'Me too,' said Trisha.

'Bring them along,' I told them. 'The more the merrier. We'll have a party. You can all bring a man along, I don't mind. I just want to go back to The Oasis again, because I think I might like it this time.' I really rubbed it in, making them feel even worse about the other night. I stared at Sue, looking for some support.

She glanced at Lynne, who nodded, and one by one the others agreed.

'Good,' I said, smiling – but none of them knew why I was smiling.

On Friday evening, we all met up at The Oasis once more. We were in a different room, a larger one, because it wasn't a private party this time. All of the others had brought a boyfriend, and that make it even better. I felt a twinge of jealousy when I saw the man sitting next to Sue, his hand casually resting on her bare knee. Sue introduced us; his name was Philip, and he went and bought me a drink.

'Okay,' said Sue, 'so here we are. Happy now?'

I nodded, glancing around so that I didn't meet her eye, instead focusing on the people dancing near the stage. Sue seemed aware that something wasn't quite right, but clearly she had no idea what it was; none of the others seemed suspicious. I'd been concerned that they would have seen signs or posters proclaiming tonight's event, but the only thing which might give a clue was the red and white banner which was hung over the stage at the end of the room. It was the name of the drinks company which was sponsoring the event.

Some of the others at our table joined the dancers or went to the bar for more drinks, but I simply sat and waited, and finally the music stopped and an announcer appeared.

'Good evening, ladies and gentlemen,' he said, 'I'm sorry to interrupt the music, but this concerns five ladies who are in the audience but should be backstage.' He pulled a piece of paper from one of the pockets of his dinner jacket. 'Are these girls here?' he asked, glancing around the crowded room. Then he read out Lynne's, Rose's, Trisha's, Sue's and Jean's names.

I was watching their mystified expressions as they automatically answered him.

'Come on then, ladies,' the announcer said, beckoning to them, and hesitantly they stood up. 'The Wet T-Shirt Contest starts in fifteen minutes, you've got to get changed.'

They froze immediately, staring at each other and their escorts, while some of the audience clapped and cheered them.

They all started talking at once, arguing and protesting – the girls and their boyfriends.

'Come on, come on,' called the compère impatiently.

Lynne shook her head frantically. 'There's some mistake,' she claimed, while Rose sat down quickly, Trisha's man pulled her back into her seat, Jean took a few backward steps as though the announcer intended to drag her forcibly up onto the stage ... and Sue glanced at me.

I sat without moving, trying to look innocent. But I couldn't keep my face straight, and I put my glass to my mouth to try and mask my smile.

'It was you!' Sue accused me. 'You put our names down!'

'Me?' I said, frowning. 'I don't know what you're talking about.' Then I burst out laughing, and they all stared at me. 'You should have seen your faces!' I shook my head in amusement.

Sue sat down. 'Very funny,' she said, nodding her head resignedly. She leaned towards Philip, telling him what was going on and briefly explaining why I must have done it. The other girls glared at me.

'Come on, ladies,' said the announcer, watching as Jean, the last of the five, took her seat again. 'Don't be shy. We're all waiting for you.'

Philip angrily shouted: 'They're not coming!'

The compère came down from the stage, striding towards our table. He stared at the girls, his hands on his hips. 'What do you mean?' he demanded.

'There's been some kind of mistake,' said Lynne. 'I told you that.'

'It's all a joke,' Sue explained. 'Someone's been playing a practical joke.'

The announcer couldn't absorb this information. He held out the piece of paper towards them. 'These are your names, aren't they?'

'That's right,' Rose's boyfriend said, 'but none of them are entering your fucking stupid contest, so fuck off.'

'But . . .' The man scratched his head. He was about thirty years old, of medium build, with immaculately groomed light brown hair. He sighed, then leaned forward on the table, lowering his voice. 'Without them, there'll be no contest,' he said, staring at the men as though the girls weren't there. 'These five are half the entrants. There's a minimum of six, it's in the company rules. So the whole thing will be off.' He glanced around the room. 'And there'll be a lot of disappointed people here. I wouldn't like to be in your shoes tonight. There could be trouble.'

'Tough shit,' said Trisha's man, putting his arm defensively around her shoulder.

'You've got five girls, right?' said Sue. 'So you only need one more?'

'Yes!' agreed the compère. 'Just one of you.' He studied each of the five in turn. 'Please?' Licking at his dry lips, he added: 'Look, we can come to some financial arrangement if that's what it is.' He looked optimistically towards Sue, hoping she was going to volunteer.

'She's not going on that stage,' warned Philip.

Sue glanced at him, pushing his hand off her arm. 'What I do, or don't do, is up to me,' she told him coldly. Then she levelled her expressionless eyes at me.

I wasn't precisely certain what a Wet T-Shirt Contest involved, and when I'd put their names forward I hadn't expected any of them to enter. I just wanted some measure of revenge for the previous week's escapade; but I hadn't anticipated that I would cause all this bother.

'I'll do it,' I said quietly, under Sue's almost hypnotic gaze. I regretted my rash words nearly at once, because as they all stared at me the announcer grabbed my arm and almost lifted me out of my chair. As if in a dream, I shrugged his hand off and walked towards the stage. None of this was real, it couldn't be happening.

But almost before I realized it, I was behind the curtains and the compère was talking to me.

'I really appreciate this,' he said, 'and if I appreciate it, then the company appreciates it. I'm Tony. What's your name? How old are you? How much do you want?'

I answered his first questions but couldn't think of a reply to the third. He named a sum, which was as much as I earned in a week. When I didn't reply, Tony immediately doubled it, adding: 'That's as high as I can go.'

I nodded my head.

'Good girl,' he grabbed my wrist and pulled me to a door. 'Now go and get changed.'

'Into what?'

'It's all in there. Is there anything you want? A drink?'

I nodded again.

'Good, fine, good.'

Then he was gone, and I found myself behind the door and in a changing room. I stared, unbelieving, at the sight which confronted me – the five other contestants, half-dressed, half-naked – and it was this which brought me back to awareness as I gazed at the beautiful nude female flesh which reminded me what I'd been missing since I'd lost Carole.

One girl was totally naked, with high conical breasts

and a thick thatch of brown pubic hair; another displayed the most gorgeous backside; a couple of the others were topless, while the last was wearing simply a T-shirt which hung just above the heavenly black triangle where I focused my gaze.

A Wet T-Shirt Contest. Did that mean wearing absolutely nothing but a white T-shirt, which was emblazoned with the name of the drinks company in bright red letters across the breasts? Surely it couldn't do.

But whatever it was, as I gazed at the other girls I was certainly glad I'd come here. My nipples hardened and I felt a throbbing deep within my crotch.

Then the door opened again, and a smartly dressed woman appeared behind me. 'There you are,' she said to me. 'Get your clothes off, put these on.'

I looked at what she'd given me, a pair of white shorts and T-shirt. I did what I was told, because I wanted to stay in this room with the other five barely clad females.

Stripping down to my skimpy briefs, I watched the girls, but none of them spared me more than a glance. They were all dressed now in their uniforms of shorts and T-shirt, looking more like athletes than entrants in some nightclub contest – although the high-heeled shoes would have been out of place on a running track. As I donned my T-shirt, I wondered vaguely why they used the word 'wet' in the title, but my thoughts were on other matters. I wasn't sure why I'd volunteered to enter, but I was here now and had to make the most of it, and I began to pull on my shorts.

The woman organiser came over to me. 'A word of advice,' she said. 'You'd do better without your panties, because the line shows through your shorts.'

I'd noticed that none of the others wore a bra beneath their T-shirts, presumably for the same reason. Taking off the shorts again, I thumbed down my briefs, then pulled my shorts on once more, tugging them up and stroking my palm against my crotch as if admiring the snug fit, but in reality pressing my middle finger against my labia to give myself a moment of pleasure.

The door opened. It was Tony, carrying a tray laden with glasses. He passed them around to the contestants, giving another to the woman and saving the final one for himself. It was the same stuff we were advertising on our T-shirts.

'Okay, girls,' he said, looking us all up and down. 'The rules are very simple. I'll announce you one at a time, and you come onto the stage, then go off again, then the next girl. I gauge the audience reaction, the applause, and the best three will come back on again. The audience picks the winner. It's as simple as that. So do your best. The winner goes through to the national finals with a chance for the grand prize, but you all get a free bottle of . . .' He held up his glass, raised it in a toast to us all, then took a sip. 'May the best girl win.'

He was standing next to one of the other girls, and as he turned to leave I saw her hand reach out to touch his groin with a lingering caress. That couldn't have done much harm to her chances, I realized.

'I'll send you out one by one,' the woman organizer said, as she stood in the doorway, facing towards the stage and watched for the signal. 'Right. Candy, off you go.'

Candy was the girl I'd seen totally nude, and she hurried from the room. Half a minute later we heard a huge cheer drift through from the audience. Then the second girl was called.

Finally there were only two of us left, the other being the one who'd rubbed the compère's genitals. She was about the same height as me, with short auburn hair and although her hips were wider than mine, her boobs were about the same size, although more droopy.

'Joanne,' said the woman, and the girl disappeared through the doorway.

Now that I was alone, I picked up the other glasses which hadn't been drained, tipping the contents down my throat in record time. I heard Joanne's cheer, and then it was my turn.

I didn't feel nervous at all as I walked out onto the stage. It was simply one of those things which had to be done, and worrying about it wouldn't make it any better. At least I could console myself with the thought of the money he'd promised me, then I wondered if there was any way I could be certain I'd be paid.

I took no notice of the audience, hardly heard what Tony was saying as he walked me to the centre of the stage. There was no sign of the other girls, they must have gone off the stage at the other side. What puzzled me most was that the floor was all wet.

Tony stepped back, and I became aware of a photographer standing on the main floor a couple of yards back, his camera aimed at me.

Then it happened — Tony hurled a bucket of cold water all over me!

I staggered back in surprise, too astonished even to cry out. At last I became aware of the significance of the contest's name. The water had been aimed at my T-shirt, although my face and legs had also been splashed. But my shirt was soaked through, and it clung tightly to the contours of my body, showing every detail of my breasts. The coldness of the water had stiffened my nipples even more, and their rigid outlines and colour stood out through the thin fabric which had become almost transparent.

The audience cheered and whistled and clapped, while the photographer clicked away. I wiped some drops of water from my face, and watched them all, then turned towards Tony who was dutifully applauding me. I guessed it was my own ignorance which had led me into this and that the others had known what they were letting themselves in for.

The announcer took me around the waist and hustled me backstage, to where the other five were waiting.

'Okay,' he said, and he pointed to Candy and Joanne. 'You, you.' He nodded to me. 'And you. You're the finalists. The rest of you, go through there and get changed. Thank you very much.' He glanced at the three of us who were left. 'Same as before, okay? Only this time you're all on stage together. Don't forget to smile. Ready?'

'Yes,' said Mandy, and she gave both her nipples a squeeze. They needed it, not being very prominent.

I nodded, and so did Joanne – and a moment later Tony stroked her curvy bottom. Then he went back onto the stage, calling us up one by one, and I listened as the other two were drenched and cheered in turn. As he called my name, something attracted my attention. It was a fire bucket hanging on the far wall, and immediately I walked over to it. It might have been filled with sand, but instead it was full of water.

I removed it from its bracket and began to carry it towards the stage, picking up momentum and running as I heard my name called again. And then I arrived on the stage, saw the other two girls, the announcer at the far side, and I flung the contents of the bucket at him, catching him squarely on the head and chest as he tried to duck. Tony backed away and stepped out of sight, and I became aware of the cheers and laughter which were far louder than any others so far this evening.

Candy and Joanne watched me with amazement. My run had carried me past them and to the bucket of water which had been prepared for me. I discarded the fire bucket and lifted the other one, wondering what to do. From the corner of my eye, I saw Tony, but he stepped further into the shadows when he noticed I had another full bucket.

I stepped to the edge of the stage, and swung the bucket backwards, watching the looks of dismay from the people sitting in the front tables as they threw up their arms and leaned away, thinking I was going to hurl the water all over them. But instead I raised the bucket high into the air, then tilted it, pouring the contents all over myself, soaking my hair, drenching my clothes, wetting every inch of my skin, relishing the gales of applause from the audience.

Then Tony appeared by my side, taking the bucket from my hands. He wasn't quite as wet as I was, though water dripped from his no longer perfectly styled hair. He glared at me through narrowed eyes, but I observed a glint of humour and after a few seconds he smiled briefly.

He put the bucket down and spoke into his microphone. 'Ladies and gentlemen,' he said, wiping his face with his sleeve, 'I have great pleasure in announcing that the winner of this heat of the Wet T-Shirt Contest is – me!' He paused to allow the burst of laughter. 'No, seriously, ladies and gentlemen, tonight's contest has been very close – not to say unusual. I think they all ought to win, and they've each won an entry in my address book already, but the third place goes to – Candy!'

Candy accepted her applause, and left the stage at the compère's nod. Tony came to stand between me and Joanne. It was obvious who ought to have won: My soaking wet outfit proved beyond any doubt that I had a much better figure than Joanne's, and the audience had already given me the biggest cheers of the night for my performances with the two buckets. But it was equally obvious to me which one the announcer wanted to win.

'This is going to be tough,' he told everyone. 'I think you ought to remind me just how good you think our two beautiful finalists are. How about another big cheer for Joanne?'

I noticed him prod her in the ribs with his elbow. The girl glanced at him doubtfully, but he nodded. Her applause was beginning to fade, but then she took off her T-shirt and stood topless, raising her arms to lift her breasts, and the clapping and cheering was renewed, doubling in volume and intensity, finally dying away.

And then the announcer called on my supporters to show their appreciation.

A voice in the crowd shouted out: 'Strip!'

More people took up the word, turning it into a chant: 'Strip, strip, strip!' They began clapping as they yelled for me to disrobe.

I stared out into the audience, searching for Sue's face, because what I did next was for her.

I peeled off my dripping T-shirt, swirling it around my head and then flinging it into the audience – who shouted and clapped even louder, with far more enthusiasm then they'd given Joanne.

Having gone that far and enjoying the crowd's reaction so much, I simply pushed down my shorts and stepped out of them. I stood in front of the massed throng of strangers, naked except for my shoes, my feet braced twenty inches apart. My nude body glistening with drops of water as I raised my arms above my head, clenching my hands together in a victory salute.

Needless to say, I won. Joanne wasn't prepared to go to the same lengths as me. Although I'd stripped off for Sue, she'd never know it, and it was the males in the audience who vented their approval of my display and voted me so noisily into first place.

And as I stood there, revelling in their enthusiastic response, I closed my eyes, clenching the muscles of my cunt and triggering off the first orgasm I'd ever had without some sort of physical stimulation. It was as though everyone in the crowd had been fucking me, all the men, all the girls, because it was they who had stimulated me – just by being there and reacting so positively to my body.

For a moment, as I spiralled higher and higher, then closed my legs to prolong the spasms, I wondered about the effect that my nude body must have been having on the watching males, aware that I was being carried aloft by their combined sexual power.

Then I felt something being draped over my shoulder, and I opened my eyes as Tony hung the winner's sash across me, using the opportunity to stroke the palm of his hand across my right breast, while the fingers of his other hand brushed against my pubic hairs as he pretended to adjust the sash. It was the first time a man had touched me in either place, and because I was still trembling in the last internal throes of orgasm I didn't mind. It was worse when he kissed my cheek a minute later, after making a short speech which I wasn't listening to. He presented me with a bottle of spirits, and I wiped my cheek with the back of my hand.

I was watching the crowd as I slowly recovered from my few seconds of ecstasy. It wasn't the best orgasm I'd ever had, but it was by no means the least memorable.

I could hardly believe what had occurred, any of it, from the moment I'd volunteered to join the contest right up until this instant – but I wouldn't have missed it for anything. The sash didn't hide any of my vital assets from view, hanging as it did between by breasts and over one hip.

While I gazed at the crowd, I saw the photographer again. He was still taking pictures of me. I wasn't sure I approved of this. What right did he have to do it? What I'd done had been totally spontaneous, and it ought to be soon forgotten – but photographs would provide a permanent record of my temporary lunacy.

'Okay,' whispered Tony in my ear. 'They've all had a good look. Let's go, before you catch cold.' He took my wrist and led me off the stage, although I turned and waved my prize bottle and was rewarded with a final cheer.

'You were great, girl,' Tony said, as we headed for the dressing room. 'That must have been one of the best contests ever. Keep it up and you could win the final.' I felt his hand slide down my back, towards the cleft of my buttocks.

I spun around angrily. 'Take your hands off me!' I ordered. 'Just because I won, doesn't mean I've become

72

your prize. And I've no intention of entering any more of these stupid competitions.'

He stared at me as though I was talking a foreign language, pausing halfway through opening the door. I pushed my way in, slamming the door on him. He tried to follow me, but the woman organizer was there and she refused to admit him.

Pulling off my sash, I dropped it on the floor then walked to the bench where I'd left my clothes. The other girls were almost dressed by now, and they watched me.

'Congratulations,' said one. 'That took a lot of nerve.'

'Yes,' another agreed. 'I wouldn't have dared do it.'

'Maybe I would,' Candy said, 'if I looked as good as you. You've got a fantastic body, you know.'

I nodded, although not in answer, more in thanks for what they'd said.

Joanne was staring at me. 'Well done,' she muttered, making no attempt to disguise her lack of sincerity.

'That was quite daring,' said the woman, bringing me a towel as I sat down. 'I'm still nervous about undressing when my husband's in the room, but in front of all those people . . .' She shook her head in admiration, then she began to dry my hair for me.

The number of people hadn't bothered me. When there were so many, it was hard to think of them as individuals. I'd only been concerned about one person in the audience, and that had been Sue, but I realized now that my action had been a mistake and she wouldn't understand my motivation. There would never be anything between us, and I couldn't bear that thought. The only solution was not to go back to work at the office, or else Sue would always be there to remind me of what was so near but so far. I'd have to leave, find another job; but at least I had the promise of some money from Tony. After my performance tonight, he could hardly go back on his word – although he might play up if I remained determined not to enter the final.

73

If those drinks I'd had could make me behave like that, then plenty of guys would be buying some for their girls tonight. But of course it hadn't simply been the alcohol, although I could use that as an excuse.

It surprised me what the woman said about me being so daring. The most daring part had been going on stage, that was something which would always have scared me previously. Anyone who was up in front of hundreds of people, all of them watching their every move, had to be brave as far as I was concerned. Taking one's clothes off is the simplest thing in the world, because clothes are so unnatural – humans aren't born fully dressed, and it's civilization which demands that we must wear clothing.

If it weren't for the whims of the climate, I think I'd prefer to be nude all the time. I feel much freer when undressed. People are more honest and open when they can't hide behind their clothes and pretend to be something which they aren't. All men are born free, says a famous ancient slogan – to which should be added that they are also born naked; only when we're all nude can there ever be any equality. Who would be in such reverential awe of presidents and politicians, of kings and dictators, if they were naked? But that's what the famous fairy tale, *The Emperor's New Clothes*, is all about.

'You must be pleased with your prize,' the woman said, bringing me back to the present. I opened my eyes. She was still towelling my damp hair, and I'd been leaning back against her, allowing my thoughts to drift and pretending that I was back with Carole again. 'A new hairdo at the town's best salon, and a new outfit of your choice from the top boutique.'

I sighed. So much for nudity.

'And then there's the final,' she continued. 'First prize is a three-month world holiday, and that could be yours.'

I pulled gently away from her and began to get dressed, my body was almost dry by now.

74

'I've had enough of wet T-shirts,' I said. 'I don't think I could do it again.'

'But you have to,' the woman insisted. 'It's in the rules. The winner of each heat has to go through to the finals.' She lowered her voice, glancing at Joanne who was combing her hair. 'If you refuse, then you lose first place.'

I shrugged, not caring, and finished dressing. I wondered what to do now, not fancying returning to the table with the others. All the guys would be staring at me, grinning and joking. I didn't mind them looking from a distance, they were just faces in a crowd, but I wouldn't like them to get too close. Okay, so I'd taken my clothes off – but that didn't mean I was available for the first cock that came along . . . or any cock.

But Tony seemed to think he was first in line. When the other girls had gone and the organizer also left for a minute, he marched into the dressing room, smiling what he thought was an irresistible smile. He'd changed into a smart casual suit, and though his hair was still wet it was neatly combed.

'And how's the most beautiful girl I've ever seen in or out of a wet T-shirt?' he wanted to know, leaning forward to try and kiss my cheek again.

I managed to evade his lunge, ducking away and stepping aside. 'Do me a favour, will you?' I asked.

'For you,' he said, 'anything.'

'Fuck off.' It was the first time I'd said that to anyone, never having had cause until now, but it was so easy.

Tony stopped dead in his tracks, as though he couldn't believe his ears.

'You tell him, sweetie,' I heard another voice say, and I turned to see the photographer leaning against the wall by the door and watching us both.

'Keep out of this, George,' warned Tony, turning his attention to me again.

'When do I get this money you promised me?' I demanded.

'We'll sort that out over dinner,' Tony said. 'Do you like Greek food?'

'I like Greek,' interrupted the photographer, holding up his camera and pretending to take a shot of Tony being annoyed; but I could see the cover was across the lens.

'George, get out of here!' snapped Tony impatiently.

'Why?'

'George, I'm warning you!'

'What are you going to do,' George asked, throwing in his hands in mock fear. 'Hit me? Oh, go on, please. You're so manly, so tough, so virile.'

Tony grimaced, trying to keep his temper. 'What is it you want, George?'

'I want to talk to this young lady,' came the reply. 'And unlike you, that's all I want.'

I glanced from one to the other, not really wishing to talk to either of them; but I wanted my money from one and a roll of film from the other.

'This is business, Tony,' said George. 'Company business.'

'I'm talking business, too,' Tony said defensively. 'We've got to sort out the finals.'

'That's all routine, you know it. If you've come to some private arrangement, you can sort that out later when I'm not here.'

'All he's got to sort out,' I said, speaking up at last, 'is the money he promised me for being the sixth contestant. That's the only arrangement we've got.'

'Then,' said George, watching the other man, 'I suggest you go and get the girl's money, Tony.'

Tony opened his mouth to speak, then thought better of it. Slowly, he nodded his head. Then he walked towards the door.

'She'll still be here when you come back,' George assured him. 'We're not going to elope.' He chuckled far more than his remark deserved. 'I don't blame you, sweetie,' he said to me, but made sure that the other man could hear him. 'He's not my type either.'

76

I stared at him suspiciously. 'Why were you taking my photograph before? I didn't say you could.' I held out my hand. 'I'd like the film.'

'Ha!' he snorted. 'That's a good one, I must remember it.' He sat down on the bench where I'd left my clothes earlier, looking up at me and pulling a packet of cigarettes from his jacket pocket. He was in his mid-thirties, six feet tall, very thin, almost like a skeleton covered with skin; he wore thick-lensed glasses with wire rims; his curly hair was as blond as my own, but from his dark complexion it had to be bleached; and he was dressed in denim – jeans, open-necked shirt, jacket. When I declined his offer of a cigarette, he lit one with a match, inhaled, then blew a cloud of hazy smoke out of the corner of his mouth and away from me. All the time his eyes were studying me.

I waited for him to continue speaking, and finally he did.

'These photographs,' he said, tapping his camera with the hand which held the cigarette, 'are the property of the company. Because you were in the contest, they own the copyright in those photographs of you.'

'What happens to them?'

He shrugged. 'They get pinned to the walls of the management washroom so that the executives can toss themselves off while looking at them,' he told me.

'What?'

He grinned. 'Would that bother you?'

I thought about it for a few seconds. Why should it bother me? I shrugged.

'No, they use them for publicity,' George said. 'All those boobs with the company name stuck to them, it's the image they want – drink their booze and you get laid. Though I doubt if any of yours can be used, the nude ones, because they don't have the logo on them. Pity.'

'The name was on the sash,' I reminded him. There

was no harm in pointing that out, he'd realize it when he developed the photos.

He nodded thoughtfully, still watching me. 'Anyhow,' he said, 'as you've guessed, I work for the company – on a freelance basis, which is why that jerk Tony can't fire me. If he makes trouble, he's the one who's replaceable, not me.' He took another deep drag. 'And I think we could hit it off together, you and I.'

I took half a step backwards, but George shook his head rapidly.

'No, not like that, sweetie,' he told me. 'You aren't my type either, I'm afraid.'

For a moment I didn't understand, then suddenly I did. George meant that he was homosexual. I was surprised; I'd never met one before. I had preconceived ideas of what gays should have been like, and he didn't fit the stereotyped image at all. He seemed like anyone else. But so did I, I supposed. I hardly thought of myself as a lesbian, but I was. In a way I had more in common with George than I did with most other girls.

He must have noticed the dawning realization in my eyes, because he nodded and said: 'I know I'm a great disappointment to you, sweetie, that you were just itching to have my throbbing steel-like knob inside your tight juicy quim.'

I laughed, and so did he.

'Although it's true that all I want you for is your body,' he continued. 'How do you fancy doing some modelling work?'

'For this lot?' I asked, kicking at the sash with my foot.

'To start with, yes. There's a project which might interest you. But there's all sorts of possibilities. You're obviously not shy about your body.'

'So you mean nude photographs?'

'Blondes are so rare,' George said, nodding, twisting a lock of his own hair between his fingers. 'Real blondes, which you've already proved you are. What do you say?'

I said nothing, because I was thinking. I'd already decided I had to find another job, so there was nothing to lose.

'There's a lot of money to be made if you're successful,' George added. 'You've got a wonderful bone structure, and you're the right shape for a fashion model if you want to move in that direction – and the top ones make a fortune and screw movie stars and rock musicians.'

'Don't tell me the disadvantages,' I said, grinning, and George frowned.

He dropped his cigarette on the floor and ground it out beneath his sole. 'What do you say?' he repeated.

Before I could say anything, Tony was back in the room, an envelope in one hand. He ignored George, giving me the envelope. I opened it up.

'It's all there,' he assured me.

I counted out the notes, and it was. 'Thanks,' I said, looking up. 'Why don't you take me for a drink?'

Tony straightened, smiling confidently as he preened himself, dusting down the collar of his jacket.

'I'd love to, sweetie,' replied George, who was the one I'd been looking at. 'But just one, I don't want you getting me tipsy and taking unfair advantage of my body.'

Tony watched dumbly as George and I walked out of the dressing room together.

Chapter Six

After George had filled my head with his glamorous talk of travelling the world as a model, I decided that I might as well enter the final of the Wet T-Shirt Contest. The first prize, I realized, was very tempting.

There could be no fiddling with the results this time, or so I thought, because Tony was no longer the sole arbiter of audience reaction. Three judges had been appointed – the chairman of the company, a television actor and a famous footballer; or at least he was meant to be famous, although I'd never heard of him.

But gauging the audience's response would have been the fairest system, or perhaps this is just me being a bad loser. I came third. The girl who came second went off with the actor, while I later saw the winner climbing into a chauffered limousine with the chairman. Probably it was my role to be awarded to the not so famous football player, but I managed to evade him.

The final was a far more sedate affair than the heat which I'd won, because we were given strict instructions not to strip off, not even just our T-shirts – obviously the judges had never seen any bare boobs before, and no one wished to offend them.

Third prize was a useful amount of cash – equivalent to three months' pay where I used to work – so I'd done pretty well out of the liquor company. And I still hadn't touched the bottle which all the contestants had won the first night a month before. I'd considered giving it to the girls in the office as a farewell present; but there was no farewell, because after the contest I simply never went back there.

When I'd dried myself off and finished dressing, George was waiting for me. He'd been out in front earlier with his camera, but today was the first time I'd seen him since we'd gone for a drink together and he'd talked about modelling. He'd told me we'd meet again at the final, and this was one of the reasons why I'd come. Even had I been last in the contest, I'd have lost nothing; my fare to the city and hotel expenses had all been taken care of by the company.

'Hello, sweetie,' he said. 'Sorry you didn't win.'

'I didn't fancy the first prize,' I told him.

'The chairman?'

I nodded.

'I know what you mean,' said George. 'I preferred that footballer myself. I really go for the sporty types.' He licked lasciviously at his lips.

'And who needs a trip around the world when you've promised me fame and fortune?'

'You've thought over what I said?' George nodded in answer to his own question. 'That's good. Let's go for the most expensive meal in town. The company's paying, and we can discuss it.'

Which was what we did, going to a very swish restaurant for the most lavish meal I'd ever consumed in my life. If George ate in such a fashion all the time, I couldn't understand why he was so slim. A couple of meals like that each week and I'd soon lose my figure. We talked about all sorts of things, and I was able to relax and enjoy myself in George's company because there was no sexual pressure on me. It was only at the end of the meal that we finally began to discuss photography and modelling.

'I'll need to take some test shots of you for a portfolio to show the marketing people,' George said, as we sat with our coffee and liqueurs. 'We can do that tomorrow if you haven't got anything planned.'

'Only sightseeing,' I said. 'I've never been here before. So it's all new and exciting; it makes where I come from seem so dull and outdated.'

George shrugged. 'I've lived here all my life, so I prefer it when I go to small towns. They're not so cold and inhospitable, they've got more character.' He shrugged. 'I suppose it depends what you're used to – the grass is always greener somewhere else, they say. And speaking of somewhere else, have you ever been to the Caribbean?'

'You must be kidding,' I laughed. 'I've never even been out of the country.'

'Then you'd better get yourself a passport soon, because we're flying out to the Caribbean next week.'

I laughed again, but George didn't. I studied his expression and I could tell that he was serious.

'You mean it, don't you?' I said.

He nodded, draining his coffee and then lighting a cigarette.

I waited impatiently for him to finish this ritual. 'Are you going to explain what you mean,' I asked, 'or do I have to guess?'

'You're going to become a calendar girl, sweetie. Does that appeal to you?'

'Tell me more,' I insisted.

'The company's issuing a calendar this year,' George explained. 'It's sent out free to all their customers – bars and retailers all over the world. The location is the Caribbean, I'm the photographer, and we're taking four girls. I've already signed up three photographic models and I want you to be the fourth. There was some talk of the winner of tonight's contest being given the job, but I can handle that. What do you say?'

'What's the catch?'

'You get flown to a Caribbean island, stay in a luxury hotel, go swimming, diving, surf-boarding, sunbathing while I take photographs of you. You get paid a lot of money.'

'What's the catch?' I repeated.

'It's hard work, it's boring.'

'You ever tried working in an office?' I asked.

'So you'll say "yes"?'

There was something wrong here. It sounded far too good to be true. I twirled my empty glass between my fingers, wondering why George really wanted me to go. I couldn't think of an answer, so I asked him.

'Why do you really want me to go?'

'So that when you're famous and successful you'll be able to say it was old George who discovered you.' He laughed disparagingly. 'No? Well, it's because I want to do a good job on this calendar and you match exactly my vision for the project. It's as simple as that. There won't even be any cunt shots, it isn't the right image, just tit and bum.'

'I'm not bothered about that.' I'd got over my earlier resentment of George taking those nude pictures of me, because what was a photograph after all? It was only a piece of paper.

'Then what's the problem? If you think you're flying out to a desert island with a randy photographer, then you're right. I can't wait till I see those plump little native boys again.' George grinned. 'Why do you think I chose the Caribbean?'

'You chose it?'

'The company thinks they chose it, just like they think they picked the girls for the trip – the same way they'll think that you were their choice. It's hard work, but it's fun. Come on, sweetie, all you have to do is say "yes" '

'Yes,' I said.

Ten days later I was lying on a white Caribbean beach wearing nothing but the brief lower half of a bikini, sipping at an iced glass of the product we were promoting while George took my photograph – and a dozen other people clustered around us.

All of them were involved in producing the pictures for the calendar. I'd imagined that it would be just George and the models flying out to the island; but that was only the beginning. George had an assistant, and the assistant had an assistant. There was a guy to handle the lights – even under the brilliant sunlight we needed lights – and he had an assistant. There was a girl for our hair, a girl for our makeup, a girl for our costumes, and she had the easiest job of all because of how little we wore. A few times we'd have visitors, a representative from the advertising agency or the company would appear for a few hours then fly back again. They must have spent a fortune just to come up with twelve pictures for the final calendar – which worked out less than one a day, although to get these dozen George took hundreds and hundreds of photographs.

I'd been lying in almost the same position for hours, my body shaded from the blazing sun by a huge parasol, while George took endless photos and my glass was refilled – not because I'd been drinking the stuff, but because the ice kept melting in the heat. And all the while I had to look as though I was having the time of my life.

The other three girls were professional models, although I discovered that the one called Vanessa had only been working as such for three months, and they all had suntans from recent work in the Mediterranean and even Australia. They had to be careful always to sunbathe nude, because a bikini line would lose them work. I had no such problem, my skin being equally pale all over at first. But whenever they had the opportunity, the other three would strip off completely and soon so did I.

They had no inhibitions about anyone seeing them. The only similar experience I had had was in the first T-shirt competition, but the circumstances had been unusual then and I'd also been a bit drunk that night. I soon got used to the calendar crew watching me as I posed – that was work, therefore different – but it took longer to ignore the stares of complete strangers who might only be a few feet away.

The other two girls' names were Sandra and Debbie, and I got on very well with them all. At first I thought they'd resent me as an outsider, but they were full of help and advice, as though we four were allies against the rest of the team.

The three of them were so gorgeous and attractive that I couldn't understand why I'd been chosen to join them. Evidently George saw something in me that I wasn't aware of at the time, and it was an honour to be considered in the same class as the other three. Sandra, Debbie and Vanessa were the most beautiful girls I'd ever met, they looked good from every angle; they didn't need makeup or elaborate hair styles – or clothes. They were models because of their loveliness; their faces and figures were their fortunes.

Naturally enough I fell in love again. This time it was with Debbie, or to be more precise I fell in love with her cunt.

Debbie was a tall willowy girl with high thrusting breasts and jet black hair which hung halfway down her back. But her cunt was completely hairless, and the first time she stripped off in front of me I couldn't keep my eyes off her unthatched pubis. It looked so beautiful and tasty I had to restrain myself from licking my lips, but there was no way that I could prevent my inner labia beginning to swell and moisten at such a marvellous sight. Some day, I resolved, I'd shave my own twat.

This was the first night that we arrived, and she and I were sharing a room. Debbie couldn't fail to notice where my attention was directed, and she sat down on her bed opposite me and glanced down at herself, lightly touching her bald mound.

'It turns a lot of men on,' she confided.

I could well imagine that it did, because it was certainly turning me on.

'I've had it like this for a long time,' she added, 'and quite a few guys have told me that it's better than getting hairs in their mouth.' She smiled as she remembered. 'But I've got to insist that they have a close shave, too, or else their bristles can be quite painful.'

85

I continued undressing, making sure that she got a good look at my body.

'But I think if my pubes were like yours,' she said, studying me, 'I might have kept them. You blondes are so lucky.'

I'd had that said to me before. Most recently it had been George who'd commented on my colouring.

'A big black hairy triangle always seems so funny looking,' Debbie continued, 'as though it doesn't belong there. But with your pale hair and pale skin. . .' She shook her head, sighing.

We were tired after the journey and went to bed soon afterwards. I lay awake for a long time, my whole body aching for her, but this wasn't the right time to make a move. It was too sudden, and we would have two whole weeks together for me to choose the right moment. I lay with my finger touching my clitoris, but only when I was sure the other girl was fast asleep did I allow my fingers to start their magic work. I fantasized about Debbie as I masturbated, imagining her long black hair cascading across my thighs while her head was between my legs, my own mouth and lips and tongue moulding themselves into the softness of her hairless cunt. I tried not to make any noise, biting on my pillow to stifle my orgasmic cry when I came. Then I started all over again, rocking myself to sleep.

But I never did get a chance with Debbie, that being the only time we shared the room. Every other night I was alone, because she sneaked off somewhere – presumably to fuck one of the guys in the team. Everyone was doing it, I discovered. The three models and the other girls in the crew were moving from bed to bed every night. George and I were the only ones excluded from this game, although I had several propositions. The photographer, meanwhile, would be off on the prowl every evening after dinner.

Debbie and Sandra and Vanessa had difficulty understanding me.

'Don't you like fucking?' asked Debbie.

I shrugged.

'But everyone knows what these excursions are for – sun and sea and sand and . . .' She frowned. 'What's the other thing?' Then she grinned. 'Screwing's part of the job, how we unwind in the evenings. There must be someone here you fancy.'

She was concerned that I was missing out on the fun, but there was no way that I could tell her who I did fancy. I'd heard the way they talked about George behind his back, even though it was obvious that they all liked him. So I remained silent.

'I couldn't get used to it at first,' said Vanessa, 'but I soon did. It's great. I don't want the same boring prick in my snatch every night. Variety is the spice of life. So taste life – lick a different dick a day!'

They were all watching me, waiting for an answer. We were sitting nude on the beach, while George organized the unit for a rear and side view shot of us silhouetted against the giant red setting sun.

'I'm a virgin,' I said, and they all laughed as though it was the funniest thing they'd ever heard. I'd only told them because I knew they wouldn't believe me.

'What's that?'

'Never heard of one.'

'I thought they were extinct.'

'Okay,' I said, 'then I'm a lesbian.'

Their response was equally as amused and disbelieving.

'Come on,' said Vanessa, 'tell us the truth. Who did you have to fuck to get this job?'

'George,' I told them.

They glanced at one another, then without warning they jumped me, grabbing hold of my arms and yanking me towards the edge of the sea and dragging me into the water, tripping me up and falling on top of me.

We collapsed into a giggling heap of bare boobs and buttocks, of thighs and twats, rolling about in two feet of ocean. I managed to seize hold of Debbie's ankle, pulling her through the water, spreading her legs and gazing into her forbidden pink cleft. Then Vanessa clutched hold of my thigh, tugging me down with a massive splash.

I became aware of more splashing close by and I glanced around to see George plunging through the surf, the motor drive of his camera whirring as he photographed us.

'That's great, sweeties!' he yelled enthusiastically. 'Keep it up. More. More. That's it. Get really into it. Great. More.'

As he spoke, he beckoned to his assistant, who ran into the sea and handed him another camera. With hardly a pause he was shooting us again as we frolicked naked in the shallows, diving on one another, two of us ganging up to drag a third girl under the surface, scrabbling frantically for breath, but unable to stop laughing despite the water in our mouths, eyes, ears, cunts.

Over and over we rolled, kicking up the sand and water at each other, then flinging ourselves against the nearest nude body, tugging slender limbs, toppling backwards and then finally dropping in exhaustion, panting, water dripping from our hair and down our breasts.

George was waist deep in the water, still fully dressed, still photographing, shouting at us not to stop.

Debbie glanced at me, I glanced at Vanessa, Vanessa glanced at Sandra, and without a word we launched ourselves at George. He saw us coming and tried to step back.

'The camera!' he shouted. 'Mind the camera!' But even as he was warning us, he kept clicking the shutter.

Vanessa and I reached him first, hauling at his legs. As George fell, he kept one arm raised to hold his camera out of the water, while his other hand held his glasses tight against his face so he didn't lose them.

Sandra seized the camera and hurled it towards George's assistant as the photographer sank below the surface. The guy caught it then swiftly fled to the shore out of our reach.

George fought frantically and desperately as we began to strip him.

'Don't you dare!' he screamed, between gulps of water. 'You'll never work again! Any of you! Get off me! Let go!'

Somehow he managed to twist half away, leaving Debbie and Sandra holding his shirt. I hadn't been concentrating on the man, instead focusing my attention on my nubile companions. But the other three were taking this too seriously now, I realized; so I pretended to stumble, managing to bring Debbie down beneath me, my hands caressing her nipples as I feigned an attempt to save us both. Then George was free and wading back to the beach.

'Okay, sweeties,' he said, both in anger and relief, as he reached the sand the turned to face us. 'Fun's over, out you come.' He used his fingers like windscreen wipers on his spectacle lenses. Looking beyond us, he noticed that the sun had begun to melt into the ocean. He shrugged. 'Tomorrow is another day – and another sunset.'

Sandra followed George out, carrying his sodden shirt, and I admired the sway of her nude buttocks as she strode onto the beach. Vanessa had begun swimming parallel to the shore, her elegant arms and shapely legs propelling her in an easy crawl. And Debbie was floating on her back, only her face, the tips of her breasts and her hairless mound above the surface as she drifted a couple of yards away from me.

I watched her. I was sitting on the shallow sea bed, the water almost as high as my breasts, the flow of the current gently rocking me up and down. The ocean washed against my open labia, and I didn't even need to use my fingers to start bringing myself off. This was far better than any douching, the natural rhythm of the warm surging tide in perfect harmony with my own internal pulses. I kicked myself gently upwards, thrusting out my arms to balance properly, and then I was floating on my back, edging towards Debbie, my legs wide apart.

We bumped into each other, and she cried out in surprise. I spun around, colliding with the girl again and reaching out for her as if to save us both from going under as we rolled over together. As soon as I wrapped my arms around her naked body, feeling her breasts and hard nipples against mine, gripping one of her thighs tightly between my legs, I came.

Debbie held me against her, trying to steady us both, gazing curiously at me as I opened my mouth and gasped in ecstatic joy.

'Are you all right?' she asked.

I managed to nod my head.

'That's good,' she said. 'For a moment I thought you were drowning or something.'

She was almost correct; I'd been drowning in a flood of pleasure. It was obvious that she didn't suspect what had really happened. We found our feet, then made our way back to the shoreline together. There were four days more before we were due to fly home, away from this tropical paradise, and I knew that I'd never be as close both physically and emotionally to Debbie as I had been a minute earlier. But that no longer mattered, because I'd reached my ambition – although she didn't realize it, the girl had helped me achieve fulfillment.

It had been an enjoyable experience, and it would continue in my mind as a happy memory. When I look back, my life is documented by such fondly recalled moments of joy. I try to forget all the rest, because who wants to remember the bad times?

I remember the Caribbean trip as being one of the most important periods of my life, perhaps even the most important of all.

Chapter Seven

The next evening we were again in position at the edge of the ocean as the sun went down while George used up several rolls of film, yelling at us all the time to shift one way or the other, to bend over slightly, or to lean back so that the curves of our breasts showed up against the sun and the sky.

'Okay, sweeties,' he announced as the sun finally sank beneath the horizon, 'let's call it a day.'

His assistant and his assistant's assistant began to put away the equipment, while the photographer came over towards us.

I wondered whether he might at last say something about the incident when we'd tried to strip him. No one had mentioned it since, although perhaps that was because today had been very hectic.

I'd more than enjoyed cavorting amongst the waves with the other three girls, and George had used the opportunity to capture those few brief minutes in his camera. But what good were those pictures to him? They couldn't be used for the calendar.

'We've only got two days left,' he told us as we began to dress. 'And there are still two final shots.'

'No problem,' Debbie told him.

'Possibly not,' George replied, 'but we've got to make the most of the good weather. If there is any more good weather.'

'What do you mean?' Vanessa wanted to know.

'There's a hurricane sweeping through the Caribbean,' said George, 'and there's a fair chance it could turn and head in our direction.' He shrugged. 'So I want to get as much done tomorrow as possible. We'll do that shot with Debbie and Sandra by the hotel pool tomorrow morning. In bed nice and early tonight please.'

'Who with?' Sandra asked, smiling.

'With an early riser,' George told her. Then he realized what he'd said. He thumped his forehead with the side of his fist, while the three other girls giggled in amusement and made various ribald comments.

George watched them, shaking his head as if in disbelief, then he glanced wryly at me. 'I'm glad you'll look as young and fresh as ever tomorrow, sweetie. Not like these old hags here. It's lucky all they ever have to do is lie around and have their photographs taken, they'd never have the energy for anything else. They lie down at night, lie down during the day.' He shook his head in mock sorrow. 'I despair of this younger generation.'

Debbie, Sandra and Vanessa pulled faces at him.

'You look better like that,' George remarked. 'Hold on, I'll get my camera.'

We finished dressing and began heading back to the vehicles parked on the single track road beyond the beach. But George put his hand on my arm, holding me back while the others went ahead.

'I've got to go to the other side of the island tonight,' he said. 'I want to scout out a location for the final shot. Do you want to come with me?'

It was more tempting than being stuck alone while the rest of the crew were busy fucking each other.

'Okay,' I agreed. 'But how can we see anything in the dark?'

'That's the idea,' George said, and we began walking towards the road. 'I want the final shot set at night – a single nude lit by moonlight. You'll be the model, too, although I don't want you to tell the others yet. It won't really be moonlight, but the lighting will seem like that. There's a full moon tomorrow, and you'll be on top of the island's highest point with the sea in the distance. A full length frontal nude, but because of the light we'll have none of that nasty pubic hair. Your long blonde hair will be the focus of the shot. I can see it perfectly in my mind, and I want to see if the location will work for tomorrow.'

'Sounds wonderful,' I said, and it did. But I wondered whether George would have given me the final picture if I hadn't agreed to go with him tonight. That might have been unfair. It depended which had the most priority – a blonde or the lack of pubic hair. I was the only blonde of the four models, but Debbie would be the easiest to shoot if he didn't want any cunt hairs . . . not that he'd want her slit visible either.

'That's settled, sweetie,' he said. 'We'll go off now, have a meal on the way, then see what this place is like at midnight. We'll be back late, but you won't have to get up early tomorrow.'

'Can't we go back to the hotel so I can change?'

'You look fine. We don't want to waste time.'

I didn't think I looked fine. All I was wearing was a pair of old jeans, a woollen sweater and a pair of sandals. I didn't even have any underwear. Despite the heat of the day, it soon became cold when the sun was down and I needed some other clothes if we would be out late; and if we were going to a restaurant, I'd have preferred to have a better outfit. But George was the boss, so I merely shrugged in resignation.

He commandeered one of the cars, told the rest of the crew where we were going – not that anyone particularly cared – and we drove off one way while the other vehicles headed in the opposite direction. There was no need for a map, because the island was so small that there were very few proper roads. The one we were on led away from the capital and straight through the hills towards the other side of the isle.

The road became worse the further we went, and George had to slow down because of all the holes and cracks in the surface. It was clear that we were heading away from the tourist area, and we hardly saw any other cars. After a while we came across a small hotel, parked outside then went in for a meal.

We had a couple of drinks first, two bottles of wine while we ate, and a couple more drinks afterwards.

'It was only three weeks ago that you took me for that first meal,' I said as we sat at at table in the bar. We'd been on high stools before the meal, but by silent agreement we'd now chosen less precarious seating. Having drunk so much, it wouldn't have been safe to risk stools.

'Is that all, sweetie?' said George. 'It seems more like twenty-one days to me.' He grinned. 'But this was a much better meal at a tenth of the price, right?'

I nodded in agreement.

'Are you enjoying yourself?' George asked. This was about the only time the photographer and I had been alone together since we'd arrived in the West Indies.

'Very much,' I told him truthfully.

'You get on well with the other girls?'

'Yes, of course. They're fun and I've learned a lot from them.'

'They're a randy trio,' said George. 'Which is why they go on these trips so often. But I've noticed that you haven't been . . . er . . . indulging in similar carnal activities. That's something you haven't learned from them.'

Everyone else in the team knew about my lack of sexual activity. Amongst so few, the story had soon spread. In their eyes I'd become an ice cold frigid blonde.

I shook my head. 'I have to be in love,' I sighed, but I was unable to surpress a smile.

'And Debbie's the one, isn't she?' said George.

I stared at him, startled. There was no point denying it. 'Is it that obvious?' I asked.

'Probably only to me. I'm sure Debbie is unaware of your feelings for her.'

I said nothing, because there was nothing to be said.

'I could stay here all night,' George said, staring into his empty glass. 'But there's work to be done. Shall we carry on our journey?'

'Is that wise? You've had a lot to drink, George.'

'But not enough. I'll buy a bottle of rum to take with us. Don't worry. Never drink and drive, I always say – in case you spill any!' He laughed, then called over the barman. 'Don't worry, sweetie. There aren't any other cars on the road, so we'll be okay.'

Three minutes later we were on our way back to the car. I noticed that it was more windy than it had been a couple of hours ago, and the sky was overcast. The moon and stars could no longer be seen through the dark clouds. It would have been futile to point this out to George, because he'd have thought I was trying to wriggle out of the midnight mountaineering which he'd planned.

We climbed into the car and resumed our expedition, and I tried not to consider that I could have been back in my comfortable hotel room with a good paperback. But that was what I'd been doing every night since we'd arrived, so at least this made a change. George was driving more cautiously now, because he knew he had to; but after fifteen minutes he asked me to open the bottle of rum, and he swigged it as he drove.

The car moved slowly through the darkness, bouncing across the rough road surface and buffeted by the winds. It began to rain, a few heavy drops suddenly splattering against the windscreen. After a few attempts on the horn and indicators, George managed to find the wipers; but by then the rain had stopped as quickly as it had begun.

'Soon be there,' he assured me.

'Soon be there,' he repeated half an hour later, and by that time I was helping him with the rum. The first gulp burned my throat with its fierce rawness, but I soon got used to it.

Then to my surprise, George suddenly announced: 'Here we are.'

The car stopped, and it was so dark outside that we could have been almost anywhere. Assuming this was the place George had been heading for, I admired the way he'd managed to bring us here. I felt quite light-headed, and from the amount he'd consumed the photographer must have been at least as drunk as I was.

George climbed out of the driver's seat, and I also left the car. I realized that we were quite high, because in the distance I could make out the sea; it was brighter than the land in between, reflecting what little light there was. The wind was even stronger now.

'Up there,' said George.

My gaze followed his pointing finger, and I saw a dark shadow looming up in the sky ahead of us. As my eyes became accustomed to the gloom, I recognized it as a jagged peak of rock thrusting up into the black night.

'Come on.' The photographer beckoned to me, then started walking. He was carrying one camera slung around his neck, while his gadget bag hung over his shoulder.

I hurried to catch up with him, staring up at the bleak precipice which confronted us. Despite being drunk, I knew that this was crazy. We couldn't possibly get up there, not in the dark. It would be bad enough in the daylight and sober.

But as we came closer, I realized that the light was deceptive. The pinnacle of rock was nearer than I'd thought, and not so daunting and impossible as it seemed at a distance. There was even a path which led towards it – and a flight of concrete steps. Everything had been made easier for the tourists, for which I was grateful, because I managed to trip and stumble even on the footpath.

We made our way towards the summit, where the wind was blowing even more.

'Clothes off, sweetie,' said George, and I obeyed.

I unzipped my jeans and let them fall, stepping out of my sandals as well as the denims, then I pulled my sweater off and folded it on top of my other garment. Naked, I shivered in the sharp breeze.

At that moment the sky became for a moment as bright as day, a ragged fork of lightning abruptly splitting the darkness, and a few seconds later came the rumble of distant thunder.

George was standing opposite, watching me through his camera viewfinder. It seemed that he hadn't been aware of the lightning.

'I want the sea beyond you, there, yes,' he said. 'The moon will be behind you tomorrow night, and we'll light you from that angle. I want to take a few preliminary shots now, just you standing there. So relax, sweetie.'

I heard the shutter click. George must have been using a very fast film, because there was no flash – that came a few moments later, as a second streak of lightning illuminated the peak. The interval until the thunder was less this time; the storm was approaching us. It began to rain, huge heavy drops which fell onto my nude body.

The rain was warm, and I turned my face up towards the sky, letting the drops fall into my open mouth. My hair was blowing in the wind, my skin goose-pimpled from the chill and my nipples hard. The tropical rain suddenly poured down, and in seconds I was as wet as I'd have been under a shower. The lightning flashed, the thunder roared.

After a few seconds I wiped my hand across my dripping face and stared at George, then bent down for my clothes.

'No!' he shouted, going down on his knees and aiming the camera up at me. 'Stay there, sweetie. Tilt your head back, raise your arms to the sky. Keep turning, you're enjoying yourself. This is great! Spread your arms. Spread your legs. Point with that arm. No, the other one. Lean back. Turn around. More. More. Yes! Both arms out. Toss your head. Run your fingers through your hair. Look angry. Serious. Happy. Sad. Worried. Frightened. That's great! Put your hands on your tits, stroke them. Now to your crotch. No. Just one hand. The other to the sky. Turn around. Right around. Keep going. Move your arms. Now hang your head in despair. Now both arms high. Head raised. Yes, great!'

I did as I was told, not thinking, letting George direct me as though I was a puppet on a string. All the time his camera was clicking away, while in the background the lightning cracked across the sky and the thunder rolled in menacing rumbles. I was soaked through, and so was George.

At last he rose to his feet, and I realized that he must have been out of film. He ran his fingers through his hair, wiping his glasses with his sleeve. He shook his head and slowly smiled.

'That was,' he said slowly, 'unbelievable.'

Although neither of us knew it then, George had already taken one of the final shots for the calendar – the picture for which it became most famous. It showed me like some primitive tribal priestess, naked against the savage fury of the storm, arms outstretched, seeming to conjure the lightning from my fingertips, while the angry wind blew my wet mane of blonde hair behind me. Although I was clearly nude, the glare of the lightning illuminated only the curve of my breasts and thighs and the flatness of my stomach; my cunt was modestly shadowed, nature acting as the censor to make the photograph suitable for the drinks company's purpose. Their only complaint was that the prehistoric sorceress wasn't holding a bottle of their product in one hand, but even they realized that this would have looked ridiculous.

I picked up my clothes, slipped on my sandals. George took my hand as we raced down the steep hill towards the car, jumping inside and slamming the doors, panting for breath but laughing in drunken euphoria.

George was watching me. I was still naked.

'Nude girls and cars,' he said, more to himself than to me. 'We haven't used that image yet. But I suppose they aren't selling oil or tyres.' He held his camera up, staring at me through the viewfinder. 'No more film,' he muttered. Then he reached for the bottle of rum, passing it to me first.

I took a swig. 'Thanks.'

The rain pelted noisily, against the roof and windows of the car while the wind rocked the vehicle from side to side.

'I don't know what's the best thing to do,' George said after a couple of gulps. 'Whether I should take my wet clothes off or you should put your wet clothes on.'

I shivered. 'Put the heater on,' I suggested.

He slid the key into the ignition, then turned it. He twisted the key back, then turned it again.

'Ohhhhhh . . . shit!'

'What?'

'The car won't start,' he said, frantically twisting the key to left and right.

'Why not?'

'I'm a photographer, sweetie,' George said patiently, 'not a mechanic. How should I know why it won't start?'

I knew nothing about cars; I couldn't even drive. All I knew was that I felt cold, I was trembling, and my clothes were soaking wet.

'We'll die of pneumonia if we stay here,' I said. 'Can't we push the car?'

'All the way back?'

'Push start it,' I said angrily. 'You know what I mean.'

'This is an automatic, sweetie. We can't push start it.'

'I thought you weren't a mechanic.'

'That's right; but I did once try to push an automatic. Which is why I know it's impossible.'

'So what do we do?'

'Good question,' said George. 'Very good question. If you've got any ideas, let me know.' He raised the bottle to his lips again.

I twisted my hair, bunching it in my fists and squeezing out as much water as I could. As I turned my head, I thought I saw a light further down the road, then the swirling rain obscured it from my vision. A few seconds later, the light flickered through the darkness again.

'There's a light down there,' I said, pointing. 'It must be a car coming up here.' I began pulling on my damp clothes.

George peered out through the torrential rain. 'I see it,' he confirmed. After a minute he added: 'It's not coming any closer. They must have stopped.' He glanced at me. 'Shall we go down to them? It might be the only chance we'll get. Otherwise we'll be stuck here all night.'

I nodded in agreement. Anything was better than staying in the car, and neither of us could have become any wetter. So we left the vehicle, George with his camera bag, and headed down the road in the direction of the light, fighting our way through the sheets of rain and strong gusts of wind, until the water poured off us in bucketfuls.

It wasn't a car that I'd seen, it was a house. There was another road which forked off the route which led to the summit, and the building was tucked away on the side of the hill, out of sight of the junction. It wasn't very big, but it was solidly constructed and looked expensive.

We pushed through one of the double wrought iron gates at the end of the drive and hurried towards the front door. The light we'd seen came from a bulb in the porch. Apart from that, everything was dark.

George knocked on the door, and a minute later he knocked again, louder and longer. A light came on inside, and a few seconds later the front door opened slightly.

'Hello,' said George. 'Sorry to disturb you so late, but our car has broken down. Can we use a telephone to call up a garage?'

The door opened wider, and a middle-aged man wearing a dressing gown stared at us in amazement. He shook his head in bewilderment. 'A garage? Where the hell do you think this is? There aren't any garages around here.' He spoke perfect English, but there was a strong foreign accent to his voice.

'What about a taxi?' asked George.

The man laughed, shaking his head again. He stepped back. 'You'd better come in,' he said, which was what we did. 'Celine!' he called. 'Have you got a couple of towels for our visitors?'

A plump woman of about forty appeared from a doorway along the hall, then vanished again. When she reappeared she was carrying two bath towels.

'You best come through here,' she told me, giving George and me one of the towels each, and I recognized her accent as French.

'Thanks,' I said, and I followed her through into the front room, towelling my hair as I did so. I could hear George still questioning the man behind us.

'If there isn't a taxi, can I use your phone? I must contact my colleagues.'

'The phone isn't working.'

'Lines down because of the hurricane?' George asked.

'Hurricane?' repeated the man, and he laughed briefly. 'What hurricane? This is nothing. You just wait and see what it's like when there really is a hurricane!'

'Then why isn't the phone working?'

'I don't know. This isn't the centre of Paris, my friend. We can't expect the same kind of facilities.'

The two men came into the front room. I had the towel wrapped tight around me, to keep myself from shivering. The French man stared at me.

'A glass of cognac, I think,' he remarked. 'That is what you two need.' He walked to an intricately carved wooden cabinet in the corner and opened a bottle of brandy, pouring two glasses. He hesitated, then tipped more brandy into another two of the huge glasses which were almost large enough to keep goldfish in. All four of us sipped at our drinks, and I could feel the strong liquor warming my throat and the heat spreading through my body.

After we'd both said thanks, George wanted to know: 'But if there isn't a telephone, what can we do?'

'You must stay here,' the woman told him. 'We have a spare bedroom. Everything is prepared, because my son and his wife arrive tomorrow afternoon.'

'Correct,' agreed her husband. 'And in the morning perhaps the phone will be working and the rain have stopped, and you can obtain mechanical assistance – or if you are in a hurry, then we can summon a taxi from the capital.'

'But . . .' George began, then he shrugged, realizing that there was no way of getting the car started or returning to our hotel tonight. 'This is very kind of you, but we can't possibly accept your offer.'

I stared at him in disbelief. What did he mean?

'That is up to you, my friend,' the man said. 'If you wish to walk back in the rain and stay in your car all night, then of course you may.' He glanced at me. 'And you, young lady?'

'I'd like to stay here,' I told him. 'Thank you.'

I noticed George glance at me, and suddenly I realized what the problem was – that we'd have to share the same bedroom. Or at least George saw it as a problem, although I couldn't understand why.

'We'd both like to stay,' I continued, taking the initative. 'George is worried about his car, that's all.' I introduced myself.

'Pleased to meet you both,' said the man, shaking George's hand, then taking my own and raising it to his lips in a gentle kiss. 'My name is Louis, and this is Celine, my wife.'

'Is enough talk, Louis,' said the woman. 'You not see poor girl is exhausted? All she want is get out of wet clothes and go to bed. We can talk in morning.'

102

'You go ahead, sweetie,' said George. 'Get some rest. I'll sleep on the sofa here so I won't disturb you.'

Louis watched him, then stared at me before glancing back to George. As I left the room I heard him say: 'Don't worry, my friend. It's a very big bed, and the walls are thick.' He laughed again, and then came the sound of him slapping George's back. I wished I could have seen the photographer's expression.

'Bathroom through there,' said Celine as she led me along the hall, nodding to a door opposite the one she opened. She leaned inside and switched on the bedroom light. 'Is anything you need?'

I shook my head. 'No thanks,' I told her. 'This is very nice of you.'

She smiled and patted my arm. 'Leave wet clothes outside door, and I dry them. I see you tomorrow. Good night.'

'Good night,' I echoed, then I stepped into the bedroom and pushed the door shut.

The room was sparsely furnished, but all I was interested in was the bed. There was nothing else I wanted except to sleep. I was so tired that I could have slept almost anywhere, but the double bed, with its deep pillows and plenty of thick covers, was my idea of heaven right at that moment.

I shed my shoes and peeled off my wet clothes, putting them out of the door as Celine had asked. Drying myself as best I could, I slid between the sheets and sat up while I gave my damp hair a last towelling. I wasn't thinking of George. Where he slept was his problem.

But as I yawned and let the towel drop to the floor, the door opened and the photographer entered the room. He shut the door and leaned against it, staring at me. I fell back against the soft pillows, tugging up the covers under my chin.

'You're having that side of the bed?' George asked.

'Ye –,' I yawned again, '– ah. Are you having the other side?'

103

'If that's okay by you, sweetie.'

It didn't bother me, I was too tired to care. 'Don't look so worried, George. We're only sleeping together,' I joked, watching him.

He would have to strip off completely, because his clothes were as soaked as mine, and it was this which seemed to be making him so nervous. First he took off his shoes and socks, then his jacket and shirt, drying his torso and hair. But before he removed his pants, he switched off the light.

'George!' I said with mock severity. 'How many times have you seen me naked? Aren't you even going to let me have a peep at your prick?'

'No,' he said.

Despite my tiredness, I pushed back the covers and crept out of bed, silently making my way towards the light switch. It wasn't that I had any particular wish to see George's cock, but I was trying to get my own back. George had treated our nudity so casually, but it was obvious that he was embarrassed by the prospect of being seen without his clothes – and it wasn't even as though I wanted to take his photograph.

I reached the switch and flicked it on, but I was fractionally too late. George was almost in bed, and he managed to pull the covers across his vital area.

He grinned at me. 'Too late, sweetie.'

I shook my head, pointing to his clothes on the floor. 'If you don't put your things out, Celine won't be able to dry them.'

'Put them out for me, will you?'

'Say "please",' I told him.

'Please.'

'No.'

'Okay.' George reached for his towel on the chair next to him, wrapped it around his waist, climbed out of bed, picked up his clothes, put them outside of the door, then returned to bed, replacing the towel on the chair, then removing his glasses.

I grabbed the towel and threw it into the far corner.

'You wait till tomorrow morning,' I told him, and I switched the light off and climbed into bed. We lay at the opposite ends, as far away from each other as possible. 'Good night.'

'Good night,' said George.

I was asleep within seconds.

And I dreamed, dreamed a long languid erotic fantasy.

I was naked, wandering alone through the ice pillars and glaciers of the Arctic, cold and trembling. Everywhere was so silent and still, and I tried to run to keep warm, but my feet wouldn't react properly and so I moved in slow motion through the freezing wasteland. My breath condensed in white clouds in front of my face, and my nipples stood out defensively against the unbearable cold as my whole body shivered. I had to find some warmth or else I wouldn't survive.

In the distance I saw something which seemed out of place, and as I came closer I realized that it was an igloo. A dome-shaped house of ice, its entrance a sharp vertical gash through the curve of the wall. Without hesitating, I ducked my head and went inside, and the first thing that I saw at eye level was a shaven cunt. I stood upright inside the igloo, and Debbie was standing in front of me, equally as nude.

She opened her arms in welcome, and I moved closer to her. We embraced, holding each other tight, our bodies pressed close against each other. Breasts against breasts, pubis against pubis, thighs against thighs. Gradually we sank down, falling onto the animal furs which lined the floor, our hands exploring each other's bodies. We hadn't yet kissed, but there was no haste; we had all the time in the world.

I felt the warmth of Debbie's body, caressing her smooth supple curves with my palms. She was above me, warming me with her heat, and I clutched her buttocks to hold her close against me. Her hands stroked my breasts, then one of them slid down between us and found my cunt, slipping a finger between my moist labia

105

and softly touching my clitoris. She lowered her head to my left breast, her mouth circling the nipple, sucking and teasing it with her pursed lips, the tip of her tongue delicately licking my aureola. Then she moved to my other breast, her lips and tongue concentrating on the nipple but stimulating my whole body.

She raised her head, and at last we kissed. My lips parted, and Debbie's mouth was against mine, her tongue probing inside and finding my own tongue. Our lips rubbed fiercely together, tongues thrusting and counter-thrusting.

It felt so good to have her finger on my cunt, gently rubbing, and so I reached down for her own twat, my right hand leaving her bottom and sliding around her waist, slipping down through her wiry pubic hairs and then –

– and then –

– I opened my eyes, my hand touching the hardness of a penis as it forced its way inside me.

In the moonlight filtering through the window I saw George, his mouth locked against mine, his weight supported on his elbows as he jerked his hips to and fro. His eyes met mine, and he hesitated for a fraction, then thrust himself into me again.

I pulled my mouth free from his, gasping for breath, but otherwise unable to move.

I was being fucked.

This was what it was like to have a cock inside me, a man making love to me.

It was unbelievable.

I'd never felt or experienced anything like it. The sensation was amazing. To feel the flesh of George's cock sliding against my clit, rubbing against the lips of my vulva, stroking the walls of my cunt, was mind shattering, and my whole body glowed with erotic awareness. My own fingers, or even Carole's tongue, had never been half so fantastic.

Instinctively I began to move my hips, pushing against George, then moving with him. My arms went around his back, tugging his lean body even closer against the firmness of my nipples. I turned my head, leaning forward towards his mouth, kissing him, drawing him down so that we could kiss again. I tasted his tongue, felt the stubble around his lips, enjoyed his maleness plunging into me – and I wondered why I'd wasted so much of my life in avoiding such a totally hedonistic encounter.

We were as one, working in perfect harmony, our bodies made for each other. My softness was complemented by his hardness. We fitted together like some precision-built machine, my eager cunt the perfect fit for his thrusting cock – because that was what nature had designed them for.

I felt the trembling deep within, the first signal of impending orgasm which promised so much. I kissed George with more urgency, urging him further into me, deeper and deeper, harder and harder, my whole body throbbing with sexual potential.

Above me I heard George breathing faster and faster and faster, and I knew that he must be about to come. But I didn't want that, not yet, because I wasn't ready. I didn't want him to stop, to leave me stranded high and dry.

I reached for his hips, trying to hold him back, but he was too powerful for me and simply kept on pumping into me, his prick stimulating every sensitive nerve ending in my vagina, bringing me to my own peak – although not quickly enough.

And then with one final deep drive George's whole body became rigid, and he sighed with ultimate satisfaction as he climaxed.

I felt his seed spurt into me, swirling hotly against the lining of my cervix – and the unique sensation spurred on my own inner contractions. I cried out in helpless ecstasy, my fingers clawing at George's back, my whole body convulsing as it shuddered with overwhelming pleasure.

And I came and came and came and came.

Chapter Eight

I never did get to see George's cock, because when I woke up the next morning he was already dressed and sitting on the edge of the bed. I lay without moving, staring at him.

George smiled wryly, then shrugged.

'Why don't you come back to bed?' I suggested. 'I might enjoy it more if I was awake from the beginning.'

'What are you talking about?' he asked.

'You know what I'm talking about. The way you fucked me last night.'

George put his hand on his chest. 'Me?' he asked in astonishment. 'You must have been dreaming, sweetie. I don't fuck girls.'

I raised the bed clothes, staring down at my naked body, pretending to check that I really was female.

'I didn't have my glasses on last night,' said George. He was grinning broadly by now. 'And whatever you say,' he added, 'I'll deny it.'

'I won't say anything if you get back in here,' I told him.

He shook his head. 'I'm properly awake now, too,' he pointed out. 'I mean it, sweetie, don't say anything. It won't do my reputation any good.'

'I don't understand this,' I said, sitting up and letting the covers fall away from my breasts.

'What is there to understand? You were cold last night, and I warmed you up. That's all. Any complaints?'

There was more to it than George implied – he hadn't fucked me just for my benefit. But I shook my head. 'No, no complaints,' I told him.

'That's what I like to hear,' he said. 'Come on, up you get. Our hosts have got breakfast ready. The phone's working, and we have to get back to work. Can't leave that lazy lot in the hotel doing nothing.'

'You've done it before,' I said.

'What?'

'Fucked girls. You aren't a homosexual.'

'I am, sweetie. I can go either way, but I prefer guys. You've tried both, so which do you prefer?'

'Let's do it again and I'll tell you.'

George laughed, leaning forward to kiss my forehead. I grabbed hold of him, trying to force his lips against mine, but he slipped away and stood up.

I'd forgotten how much I needed someone else, another body to hold against me, someone to love. Male or female, either would do – although with what I knew now I had to admit there was no substitute for a good stiff prick. Which reminded me . . .

'George,' I asked, 'will you do me a favour?'

'For you, sweetie, anything. What is it?'

'I'd like to see your penis.'

'What?' he said, as though it was the most outrageous thing he'd ever heard in his life. He shook his head. 'Anything but that. I'm the photographer, you're the model, remember? You take your clothes off, not me. What do you think I am, some kind of pervert?' He laughed, then opened the door and was gone.

And that's how I lost my virginity to a homosexual, half-raped while I was asleep – and I never did get to see those few inches of flesh which deflowered me and changed the course of my life. The photographer had done a lot for me already, but I can never thank him enough for what he did that night.

George wasn't strictly gay; he was prepared to accept whatever was available. After thinking that I was a lesbian, it was a revelation to learn that there was far more to life than simply girls . . . or really just one of them – because although I'd fantasized about other women such as Sue and Debbie, Carole was the only girl I'd ever been intimate with. Girl? She was the only person I'd been to bed with until my first man had come along, in the unlikely character of George.

He was bisexual, although his inclination was towards partners of his own sex. And now I could see how that might be the best solution. Why cut yourself off from half of the human race when it was possible to fuck all of them? If I restricted myself to one gender, either male or female, that meant I'd miss out on half of my sexual potential.

As I said, I learned a lot from George: he'd already changed my life by helping me escape from the drudgery of office life, and now he had expanded my orgasmic horizons as well.

After Celine and Louis gave us breakfast, we thanked them and were picked up by the vehicle which the car hire agency had sent as replacement, and we returned to the capital. Immediately he was back, George started working again, taking up a position on the diving board by the swimming pool for a shot of Sandra and Debbie floating prone and naked on inflatable mattresses, sipping at their drinks through straws.

I hardly bothered looking at the girls, not even at Debbie's shaven twat. Why should I torture myself in yearning for the impossible when I'd sampled other less elusive delights?

We only had two more nights in the Caribbean, but I was determined to make the most of them. I knew it was hopeless thinking of George again, but he wasn't the only available male in the crew. There were his two assistants and the two lighting men, plus the four other guys who were in the team – the pair who did the most menial tasks, plus the other two who handled the administration and finance. This didn't include all the other men in the hotel, the guests and staff. While beyond the hotel there were even more potential partners . . .

As George directed the shot, I studied the possibilities. The other eight men were clustered around the pool as Debbie and Sandra drifted across the surface.

That offered me several intriguing permutations. Old or young? Tall or short? Fat or thin? Their occupations didn't matter, because I only wanted them for one reason.

I could have asked Vanessa for her recommendations, because she must have tried them all. But I had to find out for myself, use my own judgement. The big question was: where should I start?

Even the guys who weren't directly involved with the photo sessions always hung around the girls, watching. The novelty of the models' naked bodies hadn't worn off; and I didn't blame the men at all, because I liked to look myself. There was something very aesthetically pleasing about a female nude. I began wondering about male nudes. I hadn't seen George or his equipment. In fact the only man I'd ever seen totally unclad had been that stripper a couple of months ago. It seemed much further in my past than that, because so much had happened since.

The two guys who handled the business side of the unit were the only ones not needed at the poolside. They were called Tom and Roger, and they'd both tried propositioning me soon after we arrived in the West Indies, but when I'd ignored them they'd gone in search of less elusive prey.

Now it was their turn to ignore me. We'd taken over the whole pool for the morning, and I stood in the tunnel which led to the changing rooms, out of sight of everyone but Tom and Roger. The two men were talking, standing together by the water's edge. I hadn't returned to my room and was still wearing the same jeans and jumper, so I chose the simplest way of attracting their attention – I took off my clothes and slung them over one shoulder. It was Roger who noticed me first. He was about five yards away from me, and our eyes met. Then I turned and slowly walked back along the tunnel. Without having to look around, I knew he was following me.

I went into the male changing room. It was lined

111

with benches, a row of cubicles in the centre. I walked around to the far side of the room, away from the door, taking a huge towel from a peg and spreading it on the ground. Folding my jeans into a pillow, I lay down on the floor and waited for Roger.

He found me, and without a word he pulled his T-shirt over his head and reached for his zip. Roger was an average sort of guy, with no distinguishing features; and when I'd had more experience of these things I realized that even his cock had been quite average. It was already horizontal as he dropped his pants, stiffening more and rising higher as I watched.

He knelt down between my legs, his hands stroking my inner thigh and forcing them wider apart. He didn't look at my face, simply stared at my cunt. That was okay, because neither was I interested in his face – only the rod of flesh which jutted from between his legs. His right hand came down on my crotch, the palm rotating against my pubis, the thumb pressing against my moist cleft, while his left hand reached for my right breast, kneading it and pressing hard against the nipple.

This must have been Roger's idea of foreplay, because after about ten seconds and without further preliminary, he let go and moved further back so he could lie down on top of me. His left hand came down on the ground by my head, while his right guided his shaft towards the open lips of my cunt. And then he was inside, thrusting his hips fast and furious, his hand now going to my left breast and manipulating it as roughly as his other hand had my right boob.

I closed my eyes, my hips jerking up and down to slam against his. I didn't care how he was treating me, because he was giving me what I wanted, those few magic inches which slid within my twat, transmitting the delicious tremors to every atom of my body. This was sex, pure sex, nothing but basic fucking, without such distracting niceties as kissing or affection – and I adored it.

I heard him panting, his breath coming more quickly, and then I realized that he was speaking, repeating one single word again and again.

'Bitch,' he hissed with each thrust. 'Bitch. Bitch, bitch. Bitchbitchbitch . . .'

Yet he didn't seem to be talking to me, and the word said over and over became meaningless – but just the intensity of the sound was like poetry to my ears.

And then suddenly his come flooded into my cunt, and he sank down on top of me and became still, except for his hands which gently stroked my face as his heartbeat slowed and his breathing returned to normal.

I hadn't climaxed, and I tried to rub myself against Roger's cock, but he withdrew. I opened my eyes and watched in disappointment as he stood up, and I realized for the first time that we weren't alone. Tom was leaning against the row of cubicles, watching . . . watching me.

Then I stared up at Roger, at his prick which was wilting and shrinking, no longer any use for my needs. I put him out of my mind and instead looked at Tom, short chubby Tom, and he read the message, stepping forward and beginning to strip. His cock sprung from his pants, fat and eager, ready for action, and moments later the man was down on the ground with me.

It was Roger's turn to watch, but I didn't care. All I wanted was Tom and his penis. He lay next to me, tugging me over onto my side by him, his arms stroking my body, his tongue and lips everywhere. But I didn't want that, what I needed was him inside me, and I reached for his prick, grabbing hold of it, scarcely realizing that this was the first one I'd held – my brief touch of George's tool hardly counted. I rolled onto my back again, and he was on top of me, while I rubbed his glans against my clitoris.

Yet Tom refused to be rushed. His mouth found my left nipple, sucking it tenderly before switching his attention to my right tit, while his hands stroked my

113

shoulders, my rib cage, my stomach, my hips, my thighs.

I panted, my whole body aching to feel his cock penetrating me, but still Tom held back, noisily nuzzling the lobe of my left ear, then kissing my neck and throat. My hand slid down the length of his knob, finding the hairy roundness of his testicles, examining them with my fingertips. Then I took a firmer grip on his shaft, my hand returning towards the tip, feeling the outer skin slide in my grip as I jerked his cock against my vaginal lips.

'Please,' I begged. 'I want it now. Give it to me.'

'What?' Tom teased. 'What do you want?'

'I want your cock.'

'My cock? What for?'

'I want it in me,' I breathed. 'I want it fucking me.'

'Say it again,' he ordered.

'I want you to fuck me.'

'You want my cock to fuck you?'

'Yes, yes!'

'And what can I have?' Tom asked. 'What can you give me in return?'

'My cunt!' I was almost shouting now. I noticed Roger was still standing close by, watching with amusement. He hadn't dressed yet, and he was holding his semi-limp knob in his hand, lazily stroking it as I cried out.

'Your cunt?' said Tom, his hand caressing my inner thigh. 'I can have it now, can I? What if I don't want it? There's plenty of other cunt. You wouldn't let me have it last week, so why should I take it now? What's your cunt got that the others haven't?'

I threw one arm back, barely able to answer as I writhed on the floor, my other hand still stroking the swollen tip of the man's phallus against my twat. 'Cunt,' I sighed, 'so . . . hot . . . so . . . tight . . . so . . . juicy . . .'

'That right, Roger?' Tom wanted to know, and his

114

tongue traced a line between my breasts as he turned his head slightly to look at the other man.

'I've fucked worse,' Roger commented, which I realised was meant to be a compliment.

'Shall I give it to her?' Tom asked.

Roger was holding his own cock almost erect again. 'Yes,' he said, licking his lips.

'Shall I?' Tom asked me.

'Yes,' I pleaded. 'Yes, yes, yes.'

As Tom slowly slid his shaft into me, my entire being trembled, and I was instantly transported to the same moment of imminent satisfaction I'd reached when Roger had so abruptly climaxed.

Frantically, I began rocking my hips to and fro, stroking myself against the length of hard cock which had impaled me. With agonizing slowness, Tom pulled back until his glans almost came free, then he shoved forward again, then nearly out, back in again, then out. For each seemingly endless cycle, I must have rubbed myself a dozen times against him.

My hands clutched the stiffness of his manhood, feeling the flesh as it buried itself deep into my throbbing twat, my fingers caressing the lips of my vulva and my pulsing clitoris which itched for attention.

I gasped for breath, and then without warning I peaked, the thunderous eruptions of orgasm causing me to scream uncontrollably until my lungs were empty.

And just as I was recovering, Tom's prick began to spout, his jet of spunk igniting another fiery climax within my womb, and I groaned as the inferno consumed me.

Slowly recovering, I stared up at Tom, his teeth bared, his eyes firmly shut, his nostrils flared. After a few seconds his eyes opened, and he saw me watching him. He kissed the tip of my nose.

'Why did you take so long before deciding to join the party?' he asked as he pulled free and stood up.

'I'm a slow starter,' I told him.

'But when you start up,' said Tom, 'you really go.'

I was looking at his cock, pinker now than before because of its exertions, and damp from my cunt juice. A drop of semen hung from the end of its swollen purple head, and it hung down like a glowing stalactite before finally falling free and dropping to the ground. The man's dick was gradually becoming detumescent.

Roger's prick was hardly in any more serviceable condition, although I wondered if he intended to return to carry on where he'd left off. I watched him expectantly, hoping, but now that Tom was no longer fucking me Roger had seemed to lose interest as well.

Tom began to haul up his pants, and Roger also started dressing.

'See you later,' said Tom, while Roger nodded in agreement. Then they walked out of the changing room and left me lying on the floor.

I sighed contentedly, then stretched and stood up. As I regained my feet, I felt something warm and wet trickle from my cunt and run onto my thighs. Roger's and Tom's intermingled spunk, creamy and sticky. I stepped into my jeans, pulling them up tight, rubbing the semen all over my legs and across my pubic hairs. Then I put on my sandals and sweater, left the towel where it lay, and headed back towards the pool.

Everything was exactly as it had been. Debbie and Sandra still floated aimlessly in the pool, while George balanced on the end of the diving board behind his tripod, shouting out instructions to the crew. Tom and Roger were chatting as before, and they didn't even turn their heads to look at me. Not that I was looking at them, either; my attention was focused on the other six men in the unit.

We had forty-eight hours before leaving for the Caribbean. That was one of them every eight hours, which ought to be no problem.

I went for a shower and to wash my hair, and the others were still working when I returned. In my white

116

shorts and sleeveless blouse unbuttoned and knotted at the waist, I no longer felt so over-dressed. Going to the beach, I found Vanessa asleep under a huge parasol near the edge of the sparkling sea, wearing only the lower half of a tiny bikini. I woke her, she pulled on the man's shirt she wore as a top and we went to the hotel bar for a lunch of sea food and alcohol.

The picture of Debbie and Sandra in the pool was the penultimate shot, the last scheduled one being that night on top of the hill George and I had already visited. If everything went well, our last full day would be a free day. That was assuming the final two sessions produced suitable photographs. George's first and second assistants would develop and print the shots, but if anything went wrong we'd have to work on the final day. I hoped nothing would, because I had planned a busy enough schedule already.

Before we drove to the other side of the island, most of us had the afternoon free to make up for the extra hours we'd be working when it was dark. The other girls did exactly what they'd been doing for the rest of the fortnight when they weren't fucking – lazed around on the beach. I went up to the hotel room which was being used as the photographic darkroom.

The first assistant was inside, and he opened the door when I knocked. I'd been there a few times before, because I was interested in finding out what the photographs of me were like. Perhaps it was because I was vain, or maybe it was simply that I wasn't used to being photographed. In time the novelty might wear off, as it had done for the other three.

'Hello, Steve,' I said.

'Hi,' he greeted me. 'What can I do for you?' He looked me up and down, clearly signalling what he'd like to do for me.

'A couple of things,' I replied. 'Have you developed those test pictures George took last night?'

Steve shook his head. 'Not yet.'

'Okay. In that case, why don't we fuck?'

He stared at me blankly, as though he didn't understand what the word meant. Steve was the oldest man in the team, in his forties, solidly built with a pushed in face which made him look as though he'd walked into a wall. He blinked his heavy-lidded eyes.

'You can spare a few minutes, can't you?' I asked, and I reached for the 'Do Not Disturb' sign, hung it on the outside door handle, then pushed the door shut.

The man still hadn't moved, and now he frowned uncertainly. To convince him, I unknotted the front of my blouse and slipped it off my shoulders, then pushed down my shorts. Steve had seen me naked before, but not when we'd been alone together.

'Is this some kind of joke?' he asked.

I didn't answer. 'Is something wrong with me, Steve? I know you've fucked all the other girls, so isn't it about time you gave me some of your cock?' I moved closer to him, reaching for his zip.

But he pushed my hand away. 'I can do that,' he said.

There was a single bed against the far wall, and it was covered with negatives and photographs. Steve walked across to the bed, carefully picking up all the things and setting them neatly on the floor. Only then did he start taking his clothes off, and each item he carefully folded before putting it down.

I watched, and by the time he was totally naked his long penis still hung flaccidly, and I wondered if he was going to be any use to me. Almost his entire body was covered in dark hairs – his chest and back, his arms, legs and buttocks – while his pink cock was about the largest hairless area on him.

Steve lay down on the bed, propping himself up on one elbow. 'Come on,' he said. 'I've been looking forward to this ever since I first saw you at the airport.'

He could have fooled me. He didn't sound at all enthusiastic, and his prick was equally as lively. I went over to the bed and laid down at his side, and he reached out to run his fingers through my hair.

He must have seen me glancing at his prick, because he said: 'Don't worry about that. It's a big one, so it takes longer to get up – and longer to come down. Touch it, go on, hold it.'

I did as he asked, grasping it in the palm of my hand, feeling its warmth, sensing it begin to move, the blood pulsing through the thick vein. By the time it was erect, its dimensions had scarcely increased. One of Steve's hands was fondling my breasts, bringing my nipples to their maximum size, while the fingers of his other hand wriggled through my pubic hairs. I lay on my left side, opening my legs so that his fingers could slide down towards my damp cleft, but I kept a firm grip on his prick, softly pushing the foreskin up towards its tip, then stroking it back again. His thumb rubbed gently against my clitoris, the ends of his fingers stroking against the edge of my inner labia. We masturbated each other until I could stand it no longer, I had to have him inside of me.

I pulled Steve towards me, raising my right leg over his hips and wrapping it around his waist to hold him as close as possible. He positioned his left leg between my thighs, and his cock slid easily into my lubricated vagina. And we began to fuck, our bodies becoming damp with sweat and sticking together. Steve kept steadily pumping at the same easy pace, and it was up to me to vary the stroke and pressure on my cunt by rocking faster or slower, either with his movement or against it. The only way I could tell that Steve had come was by his sudden grunt and the way he missed a single beat of his thrust. I hadn't felt his spurts, and when he kept on screwing into me I thought that I'd been wrong – then I realized that he was keeping going for my benefit.

His penis was losing its rigidity, but as compensation he brought his fingers to work on my clit and cunt lips. I'd been taking it easy until then, wanting to hold back and prolong the pleasure; but now I let myself go, allowing the total sensation of orgasm to rocket me into dizzying orbit.

When I came back to earth, Steve had pulled out and was watching me. He smiled. 'That was nice,' he said. 'Thanks.'

I nodded, unable to speak.

'I'm not as young as I used to be,' the man continued, 'so there doesn't seem to be as much juice as there was. And over the past several days I've almost been drained dry. They're real ball-busters some of those other girls. But I can honestly say you're the best I've had for ages.'

I smiled. 'Bet you say that to every piece of cunt that comes your way.'

'You shouldn't use words like that,' Steve chided. 'Cunt and fuck. They aren't very ladylike.'

I laughed aloud. Lying next to him, legs wrapped around him and twat gaping wide open after a good screwing, I certainly didn't feel very ladylike. 'You're right, I suppose,' I said, just to keep him happy. 'But they're the best words I know, explicit and to the point.'

'You'd better get dressed,' he said, rising to his knees and climbing over me. 'I've got some more work to do.' He began to get dressed. After a few seconds, I also stood up and donned my own clothes. I left while he was still dressing.

Three down, five to go.

I was like a kid with a new toy. Now that I'd discovered cocks and what my cunt was really for, I couldn't wait to try as many different pricks as possible. It was a point of honour that I had to sample all the knobs which had been through the other girls while we'd been in the Caribbean; I couldn't miss out on what they'd been enjoying. And if I succeeded, I'd be top of the league – because none of the three models or the rest of the girls had been honoured by George's tool paying them an intimate visit.

*

120

But by the time I returned to the summit of the hill that night, I still hadn't managed to increase my score. George had brought Debbie, Vanessa and Sandra along even though he'd promised me the final shot. At that time we didn't know he'd already taken the last picture the previous night. But the photographer whispered to me that he didn't want to seem to have made up his mind in advance, which was why I had to pretend I hadn't been selected and why the other three all had to strip off and pose. So far we'd all been in an equal number of pictures, either alone or with one or more of the others, so we were in friendly competition to see who'd carry off the prize of being featured in the last picture. I knew I'd won – and I also intended to become the winner when it came to fucking all the males in our group.

While the other girls got prepared and lugged the equipment up the slope, George and I went back down the hill and called in to see Louis and Celine so we could thank them again. They had visitors, their son and daughter-in-law having arrived from France, but we were invited in for a drink.

'We've come back to do the final shooting,' George told them. 'The whole crew is here, as well as the three other models.'

'You notice how there's no thunderstorm tonight,' I said. 'That sort of thing only happens to me.'

'You don't look any the worse for wear,' Louis said, his dark eyes appraising me. I hadn't looked my best last night, although in the morning I'd noticed how he'd been staring at me.

'Why don't you come on up and watch?' I suggested. 'You might find it interesting.' My glance took in the rest of his family. 'All of you.' I looked at the photographer, to make sure I wasn't out of place in issuing this invitation.

'Certainly,' George agreed. 'You might find it boring, but you're welcome to come along.'

Louis nodded thoughtfully.

'Go if you wish,' Celine told him, because she had no idea of the kind of photograph that was being set up.

George had told Louis all about it that morning, and he'd grown more and more interested; his gaze had lingered even longer on me.

'I might,' Louis muttered, and he looked at his son. 'Jean Paul?'

The younger man looked puzzled, and Louis spoke to him in French for a few seconds. He was in his early twenties, darkly handsome. I'd stared at the promising bulge behind his tight trousers, but he had ignored me, possibly because his wife was with him – a small black-haired girl who didn't say a word while we were there, either French or English. Then Jean Paul replied, also in French, shaking his head.

'He's tired after the journey,' Louis translated. 'Jet lag.'

'If you want to come,' George said, 'please do. You know where we are. If not, I can only thank you again for your hospitality.'

'That goes for me, too,' I added.

George and I shook hands with everyone, the way the French always do, then headed back up to the top of the rocky hill. The moon was full and high, and the sky was perfectly clear and full of bright sparkling stars. The air was almost still, with only a hint of light wind. It was completely different from yesterday, although if the conditions then had been the same as tonight I'd never have ended up in bed with George – and would have missed out on so much.

Within minutes of our arrival, George was in action, arranging for the positioning of the camera, the lighting boom to be erected close to the angle of the moon, the models' hair and faces properly done. Then he went through the ritual of staring at us all in turn through the viewfinder. Although it wasn't as cold as last night, it wasn't too warm, and standing around in the nude for more than a few minutes became

122

uncomfortable. Whenever we weren't in position, we'd wear a thick robe.

It was while I was posing that I saw Louis. He was standing in the shadows a few yards down the slope. I pretended I hadn't seen him, but as soon as George had taken his test shots and Vanessa replaced me, I walked down towards the newcomer. I didn't bother covering myself.

'Hello, Louis,' I said, smiling, and holding out my hand to him.'

'Hello,' he said, shaking my hand. He was trying not to stare, but didn't want to seem rude by not looking at me.

I kept hold of his hand, squeezing it. Louis glanced away, but he faced towards the top of the hill and a nude Vanessa, legs and arms spread to form an 'X' shape.

Letting his hand drop, I turned and followed his gaze. 'That's Vanessa,' I said, 'she's lovely, isn't she?'

'Not as lovely as you, my dear,' he told me, which was exactly what I wanted to hear. 'You must be cold. Here.' He removed his jacket and draped it across my shoulders; it came to a level just above my crotch.

'Thanks. Yes, I am a bit cold.' I moved a pace towards him, and his right arm went around my shoulders. I glanced up at him in the moonlight, at the distinguished grey of his hair, at the symmetry of his oval face.

'Is this what you do all the time?' he asked. 'You take your clothes off for photographers? Don't you mind?'

I answered him with another question. 'Why should I mind?'

'Don't you find it degrading, humiliating?'

I laughed. 'Of course not. I like my body, and I like to share it.'

His right hand dropped down slightly, onto the fabric of his jacket directly above the rise of my breast. I didn't react, leaving the next move to Louis. His hand

123

slipped inside the jacket, finding my breast and the hardness of the dilated nipple, stroking it with his palm. Then he pulled me against him, his lips finding mine and his tongue thrusting into my mouth. My tongue responded with equal ardour, my arms reaching down to clutch his muscular thighs, the jacket falling away from me. Behind us, I heard George calling out his instructions to Vanessa.

I pulled away from Louis, seizing his arm and pulling him into the darker shadows beneath the tall palm trees which lined the steps to the summit. He leaned against one of the rough trunks, while my hands found his zip, tugged it down, then reached through for what was hidden inside his pants. All the time his hands were sensuously stroking my breasts, the palms cupping them while the thumbs rubbed against the nipples.

Then I had his penis in my hand, feeling it swell and grow, stretching upwards, upwards, amazing me with its strength and size. Louis picked me up. He grabbed me by the waist and turned me around, pressing me up against the tree. I lost my grip on his magnificent cock, but as I tried to repossess his flesh the man ducked away, sinking down to his knees, pressing his face against my cunt, forcing my legs wide apart, turning his face so that he could more easily slip his tongue into the juiciness of my twat.

As his tongue probed and thrust, his lips rubbed and stroked, his mouth sucked and kissed, I could hardly hold myself upright. The feeling was so sensational that my whole body quivered with pleasure. I'd only ever had Carole's tongue inside my cunt, but she was a beginner compared to Louis; he seemed to know every one of the tiny pleasure zones in my vagina better than I did. In seconds he was raising me towards the ultimate pleasure, bringing me off far faster than I'd ever come before.

But just as I was about to climax, his tongue withdrew, and again he picked me up. His hands hadn't

124

been idle, having disposed of his pants. Still holding me, he leaned back to sit on the ground, then he lay on his back, pulling me down so that I was kneeling over him, my legs spread across his hips.

I didn't need any instructions. I took hold of his swollen phallus, gently levering it back so that it pointed upwards, and I lowered myself down onto the stiff rod, gripping tight between the walls of my cunt. The man's hands came up, caressing my boobs. Then I began to ride him, rocking back and forth. It was like masturbating with a dildo, except that this was the real thing and infinitely better than any artificial substitute.

My first orgasm came after a few strokes, and I threw myself back, gasping in sheer bliss, panting and groaning.

Then Louis twisted his hips, and I found myself over on my back, and he was above me, his cock sliding all the way into me, stretching my cunt and probing deeper than ever. I raised my legs, gripping him around the waist to allow him even greater access.

As he fucked me and I sensed the first tremor of another orgasm, I stared up at the moon and stars, felt the hardness of the earth beneath my naked body, heard the creak of the palm trees in the slight breeze, smelled the lush aroma of the tropical plants all around us, while I kissed my lover's throat and tasted the salt in his sweat. The universe, the world, this island, Louis, myself – we were as one.

Chapter Nine

Fucking Louis instead of one of the others played havoc with my schedule the next day – which George had decided would indeed be a holiday – but I did my best. First there was Eddie, one of the guys who did all the fetching and carrying. We were going down to breakfast, the only people in the lift. I pressed the emergency stop, and we did it standing up.

There was no way we could have taken off all our clothes, although Eddie pulled his pants down to his knees and I removed my panties. But after breakfast I met up with Don, who was the main lighting man, and although we were alone in his room he insisted that we stay fully clad. He'd only fuck me if he could shove his cock out of his zip and slide it up inside the elastic of my panties, through into my cunt.

None of the remaining three were available until the afternoon, which was when I cornered Mike, the other lighting guy. We were in the room he shared with Eddie, where I'd fucked fully dressed a few hours earlier. Mike wanted to do it dog style, with me on all fours, so that he could thrust into my twat from the rear. We did it that way; I was learning all the time.

After dinner I arranged a rendezvous with the second lackey, Graham. Fucking him was pretty normal compared to the previous three – we took off all our clothes, we were lying down, and we did it face to face, Graham on top.

By that time my twat was pretty sore after so much unaccustomed activity, and I half imagined people could hear all that spunk sloshing around inside me as I walked. I hadn't even reached orgasm in two of today's screwing sessions; I was having too much of a good thing, if there ever could be too much . . .

That left only one more. Jack. He was the assistant photographer's assistant, only seventeen years old – even younger than me. His long hair was always wild and untamed; and his complexion was as smooth as a baby's; he'd hardly even begun to shave. I'd listened to the other girls talking about Jack, and he was one of their favourites. He wasn't particularly skilled at fucking, and he always came too soon, but his cock was inexhaustible, always ready for more. Such were the stories I'd heard, and I couldn't wait to discover the truth for myself. The only problem was whether my tender cunt could take much more of this exquisite punishment.

But first I had to trace Jack and lure him away from the others, and there wasn't much time. Word had obviously spread that I'd so enthusiastically taken up the same hobby as the rest of the girls, and very successfully. Their reaction was two-sided. Now I was really one of them, but also I was seen as a rival. If I'd asked, they would reluctantly have granted me free access to Jack. Yet I didn't want that – I had to reach him my own way.

I had no chance that final evening, because he'd gone off on the town with the makeup girl. He returned too late for me, because I was exhausted by the previous day's late night and today's hectic bouts of fucking. So I went to bed early – and alone.

The next morning I found Jack packing up all the photographic equipment in the room which had been taken over as the studio. He glanced around at me as I entered, nodded hello, then continued with what he was doing. I kicked the door shut, walked across the room, then sat down on the bed.

'I'm sorry,' he said, not looking up, 'but I'm very busy. I don't have time to fuck you.'

His remark took me completely by surprise, but luckily he couldn't have noticed my startled expression. 'What makes you think I want you to fuck me?' I asked calmly.

'Why else are you here?'

'I was looking for Steve,' I lied.

'He's not here.'

'I can see that. I thought he might be back.'

'What for?'

'I want him to fuck me,' I said.

Jack paused and glanced around at me.

'I want a man to fuck me,' I added. 'Not a boy.'

He shrugged. 'That's up to you, but you don't know what you're missing.'

'Think a lot of yourself, don't you?'

'Yeah.' He grinned, and I smiled at him. 'Pity I haven't time to give you a demonstration,' he continued. 'But I'm deep enough in the shit already. If I get in any more trouble, then I get the sack.'

'So? That's not the end of the world.' I was wearing a short cotton skirt and a translucent blouse, and I sat further back on the bed, leaning against the far wall.

'I had enough trouble getting this job,' Jack told me. 'I want to be a photographer, and my brother arranged for me to work with George. He'll murder me if I lose the job.'

'Who's going to sack you?'

'George – if I don't get this gear all packed up.'

'George?' I said in disbelief. 'Come on.' George was too easy-going to sack anyone.

'You don't know him.'

I smiled, because I certainly knew George better than most people; but I said nothing.

'I mean it,' said Jack. 'He treats you girls okay; but he's a slave driver to any guy he can't fuck. But he's a great photographer.'

'What about Steve? He's George's assistant. You'll be just like him in twenty-five years, surely.'

'Not me, girl. Steve isn't even a has-been, he's a never-been. But I'm going places, and George is one of my stepping stones.'

I raised my knees up to the level of my shoulders. My skirt slid up my hips, and I opened my legs slightly.

I wasn't wearing any panties. Jack knew why I was really here, so there was no point in pretending.

His eyes focused on the blonde curls of my cunt. 'I've seen it before, remember? I'm one of the guys always around when you've been posing. So don't waste your time or mine, girl. Your job might be over, but I'm still working.'

I ignored him and unfastened my blouse, then slipped my skirt off.

Jack shook his head sadly. 'I have to sort out and file all these transparencies. Work is my priority, girl.'

I widened my thighs even more, and I knew that he must have been able to see right into my cunt through my open labia. Without a word, I started rubbing at my clit with the index finger of my right hand, while my left hand went to my breasts, massaging each of them in turn. My eyes narrowed, my head tilted back and my tongue rubbed my lips as I masturbated.

Jack's determination would have been quite admirable in most other situations. But I was convinced that he wanted to fuck me, and he could easily have spared a few minutes. He was deliberately avoiding me, perhaps as an exercise in masochism. Whatever the reason, I didn't intend to let him get away with it. I wasn't going to be made a fool of, flaunting myself in front of him like this just so that he could ignore me.

Under such circumstances I could have stroked my clitoris for all eternity and never come off, so I stopped and climbed down from the bed. I was tempted to leave, but that would have been an admission of defeat. I was here for one thing, Jack's cock, and somehow or other I intended to have it.

'Perhaps I can help you,' I suggested.

'If you want,' he said, shrugging. He was standing by a table, sorting through the transparencies scattered across its surface, looking at them all, marking them off against a list, then slotting them into different boxes.

'I have to check the numbers here, see?' he told me as I came to stand by his side.

But that wasn't quite the help I had in mind. I rested my hand on the table, moving even closer to Jack, my hip touching his. Then my hand brushed one of the transparencies onto the floor, and it fell under the table. I bent down to retrieve it, and I saw the unmistakable bulge of an erection pressing against the fabric of Jack's jeans, certain proof that he wasn't as uninterested in me as he pretended. I crawled under the table, but it wasn't the transparency I was after.

Kneeling on the ground, my naked buttocks resting on my heels, I faced Jack. My head was on the same level as his groin, and my hands reached up for his belt buckle. The man made no protest as I unbuckled the leather belt and undid the button at the top of his jeans. Then I carefully unzipped him, tugging at the soft fabric of the faded denims until they fell and left his tanned legs bare. His leg muscles tensed and relaxed slightly as he leaned further across the table and carried on sorting through the transparencies.

He was wearing a pair of tight black jockey shorts, and the tip of his cock poked up through the elastic at the top. I stroked the full length of his penis, from balls to glans, with the tip of my right index finger, then squeezed it gently through the cotton of his underwear with my hand. The fingers of my left hand fondled his testicles through the material, which was damp with sweat. After a few seconds, I let go with both hands and leaned back, wondering if Jack's determination to ignore me was more powerful than his sexual instincts.

I didn't have to wait too long before one of his hands reached down beneath the surface of the table, searching blindly for me. My head darted out, and I seized one of his fingers in my mouth, holding it firmly but not painfully between my teeth. Then I freed it, instead sucking it with my lips, drawing my mouth back and licking the finger with my tongue, letting him know what else I could do . . . if he wanted.

And he wanted it, because as I withdrew my attentions from his finger, his hands went to his black underwear, pushing it down over his hips, his thighs, his knees, his shins, letting the shed garment drop to his ankles; and with his feet he pushed off both his jeans and his pants.

For the first time I could see his naked penis, so elegant and beautiful, jutting proudly upwards, the hairy sack of his testicles drawn up tightly beneath. It was no wonder the other girls so admired Jack, because his cock was as flawless as he was. I could hardly wait to taste it, to feel it in my mouth. That was something I'd never done, of course, and the idea of fellatio had never seemed very attractive. I'd considered the theory over the past two days, ever since my ideas had been so radically altered, but I hadn't seen a prick which appealed to me until now. Jack's knob was so absolutely irresistible that I moistened my lips and leaned forward to kiss it.

I started at the base of the pink shaft, then kissed it almost to the top, my lips wetly pursed against the vertical flesh, then slid my mouth down again towards Jack's balls, my tongue flicking out beneath them towards the perineum, retreating, and the tip caressing the soft hairy skin of the scrotum. I opened my mouth as wide as I could, drawing in his testicles, washing them with my saliva, then reluctantly letting them loose again.

My hands were on Jack's buttocks, and I could feel the movement from his torso above as he tried to continue with his work. But I didn't care about the rest of his body, all I wanted was his cock, and my tongue returned its loving attention to that perfect organ, one of my hands coming around to hold it steady and at a more accessible angle as I licked and sucked its length, gradually, inevitably, working towards the purple glans and its hidden promise.

I ran my tongue around the ridge of the swollen head of Jack's prick, around and around, then licked the domed tip and probed the tiny slit to discover the first drop of fluid, pulling away so that a thin trail of spunk – as slender as a spider's web – linked my tongue and Jack's cock. Leaning forward again, my lips took over from my tongue, following the delicious contours of the glans as my mouth slowly began to draw the length of his shaft across my tongue and towards my throat.

I licked and sucked, slurping hungrily. Jack's penis felt so good in my mouth, performing oral sex for him was almost as satisfying as having a tongue in my own twat. I was enjoying giving him pleasure, because I could imagine how much he was liking what I did. And although I was concentrating on my task, I was aware that Jack was no longer sorting through his transparencies. His thighs were tense, his hips pushed forward, encouraging me to swallow him even more.

The end of his cock brushed against the soft flesh at the roof of my mouth, and I bent my neck a little, so that I could take even more of him into me. But my mouth simply wasn't big enough, although by thrusting out my tongue I could reach the base of his shaft. Hesitantly I allowed his cock to slide a few inches out of my mouth, my tongue stroking along the slightly puckered line on the underside which seemed so much like scar tissue. Before it could slip totally free, I sucked it back in again, one hand gripping its base and feeding it into my mouth, while the other cupped the testicles and gave fingertip stimulation.

After a few irregular movements, I established a proper rhythm, sucking in Jack's knob, then blowing it out again, my tongue working on the tip as it slipped into my mouth, while my lips gripped tight as it slid in and out, in and out, in and out, in and out . . .

And Jack's hips began to jerk to and fro, forcing his cock even deeper into my mouth. Abruptly he became still and although I knew what this meant, his first gush of semen took me by surprise. It splashed against the back of my throat, almost causing me to gag, and I tried to pull away. But Jack was holding himself into me as he came, and my mouth was filled with his pulsing spunk. I managed to lean back, tugging at his cock with my hands, and his final spurts dribbled down my fingers.

Then the door opened, and George walked in. He stopped in his tracks, staring at Jack, then lowering his head so that he could see who was under the table.

'Hello, sweetie,' he said to me.

I could feel Jack's semen heavy in my mouth, taste its thick blandness, sense its rich texture on my tongue. I swallowed.

'Hello, George,' I replied.

The photographer stared at George, his eyes studying the lower half of his anatomy, and he smiled. 'Glad to see you're still working, Jack,' he remarked. 'You've got about an hour.' He glanced at me. 'That goes for you, too, sweetie. We've got to check in at the airport in two hours.' He turned and went out again.

I crawled from under the table.

Jack was watching me, and he exhaled noisily. 'If that had been anyone else but you under there,' he said, 'I'd have been sacked for sure. But for some reason you're George's favourite.'

'Then you ought to be grateful I was here,' I told him. 'How long will it take you to finish? If I help you.'

'Half an hour,' Jack told me.

'Then you owe me a favour, don't you?' I said, staring down at his still erect penis. I noticed the back of my right hand, speckled with creamy white drops, and I raised my arm so that Jack could see them as well. I put my hand to my mouth, my eyes meeting Jack's, and I licked it clean.

He nodded slightly and he smiled. 'I suppose so,' he agreed, and he looked over towards the bed. I went to lie down.

The other girls had been right. Jack might have been a fast shooter, but he had staying power. He even managed to come again while he was fucking me, but I didn't care about that; all that mattered was the magnificent climax which he gave me, as well as all the minor echoing tremors which spread from my cunt to engulf my whole body.

I was as good as my word, and after our screwing session and a few minutes' rest to recover my drained energy, I helped Jack finish sorting out all the transparencies which George had taken during the fortnight.

'How would you like to be in the movies?' Jack asked me as we checked off the list.

'Aren't you supposed to say that to me before we go to bed?' I said to him, chuckling. 'That's the incentive for a fuck – the old casting couch story.'

'No, I'm serious,' he replied, pausing and watching me.

'Go on, I'm listening.'

'You're the best looking girl here, and my brother is always searching for good looking girls,' Jack explained. 'I mentioned him before. He's the one who got me this job with George. Colin, that's his name, he's a photographer, too. Same sort of line as George. But he's also getting into film making. Videos for watching at home, that sort of thing, because who goes to the movies any more? He asked me to keep an eye out for likely talent. And I think your body fits the bill, girl. Are you interested?'

'Yeah,' I said, 'maybe.' It sounded intriguing, and I didn't have anything lined up when we got back. I wondered if Colin would be anything like his brother; but meanwhile I still had Jack . . . and his cock.

'Don't slow down,' I told him. 'If we hurry, there'll be time for another fuck.'

There was – and when we returned from the Caribbean, Jack took me to meet Colin. Two days later, I was working for him.

*

I tilted the bottle of cola into my mouth, allowing the contents to pour down my throat, letting some of it trickle out from my lips and drip down my chin, dropping onto my bare breasts. My hand massaged the liquid into the upper curve of my boobs, my fingers moving lower to circle the nipple, caressing it to even greater dimensions.

My hand continued its exploration of my body, stroking the tanned flesh of my ribcage, sliding across my stomach, gliding down to the curls of my crotch as I spread my legs. Then my other hand descended the same route, holding the glass bottle. I poured a generous measure of cola over my blonde pubic hairs, rubbing it in until they were sopping wet. I stroked the inside of my thigh with the neck of the bottle, pushing it higher and higher towards the lips of my cunt, lightly brushing its mouth against the longest of my wet hairs.

I breathed heavily, leaning back against the wall and thrusting my hips forward. There was no way that I could hold back any longer, and I gently pushed the round neck of the bottle into my cunt, twisting it as I shoved it higher and higher.

'Stop, stop, stop!' yelled Colin. 'Cut, I mean.'

He stared at the ceiling in despair, then wiped his face with the palm of his hand. He was a better actor than I was, not that this was saying much. Colin wasn't as handsome as his brother, not quite so tall but more thickly-set. And whereas Jack's face was as smooth as a baby's, Colin had a ragged beard.

'Sorry,' I muttered, although I wasn't. I kept on rubbing the bottle against my swollen clitoris.

'It won't do,' Colin told me. He turned to the video crew. 'Take five,' he said, then he walked towards me.

'Why are you so . . . so hot all the time?' he demanded.

'I just can't get enough, I suppose.'

He shook his head in disbelief. 'You wore me out this morning, so what makes you so inexhaustible?'

I shrugged. Colin might once have been as potent as his younger brother – although his knob could never have tasted so delicious – but that was ten years ago. Now he could only keep his cock up until he climaxed; after that he was no use whatsoever. All he'd done for me was to bring me up to a certain level, and after that I simply wanted more, more, more. It's well known that it takes women longer to become aroused and that we can last far longer than any mere male, but like all men Colin was unable to accept this. If he was sexually satiated, he didn't see why the same shouldn't be true of me.

'Take that bottle out of your twat, huh?' he said.

I did as he asked. It was a poor substitute for a firm prick, but it was better than nothing.

'No, okay,' he amended. 'If you want to bring yourself off, go ahead. Maybe then you'll have cooled down for the next scene. I've already told you, this is all good clean fun here. We're making a video for the whole family – or almost. Something that can be distributed and sold without any problems. This is make-believe sex, just girls, no men. The viewer is the only male we're concerned with. He's the guy who imagines that he's fucking all you nubile nude women. We can't have you shoving a bottle up your twat – you've got to pretend. It isn't very subtle, I know, but the viewer has to think of the bottle as his own cock. And we like to leave a little for his imagination. It's okay putting it in your mouth, the stuff pouring out like overflowing come. It might be obvious, but it isn't as blatant as you fucking yourself with that bottle. See?'

I nodded, hardly listening. The neck of the bottle was between my labia again, gliding against my clitoris. I'd known what we were meant to be doing, but whenever I felt the urge there was no way I could ignore it. Such was the case now, and I moaned as I gave the bottle a final shove to achieve a very satisfying orgasm.

Colin ran his fingers through his hair, turning away and shaking his head.

Apart from the camera crew, there were a number of other men present. And unlike the calender shooting sessions in the West Indies, I suspected that most of them had no reason to be there. All they ever did was watch. I half suspected that Colin made as much money by charging fees to these voyeurs as he did for making his video erotica.

We were filming inside the changing rooms of one of the city's football teams, so it was a safe bet that Colin was paying off the hire fee by allowing the officials as spectators – to witness a different kind of sporting activity.

Apart from me, there were two other girls in this scene, Sharon and Rena. We were meant to be school-girls, doing the kind of thing girls did together in the school shower room – or rather what men would like to imagine girls did – helping each other off with our clothes, rubbing one another's breasts and nipples under the hot spray.

As Colin had said, no men were involved, only girls. And sex between girls was okay, because that didn't represent a threat to any red-blooded macho male. Lesbianism was just good clean harmless fun, so long as we didn't go too far – and that included going too far with ourselves as well, as I'd just learned.

My fellow actresses were very attractive, I had to admit, and none of us looked too out of place as a schoolgirl – we'd all sat in a boring classroom within the past two years. It was a pity that school had never been as much fun as making the film of our imagined romps, or else I wouldn't have been so eager to leave.

After concentrating so much energy on fucking men, it was nice for me to be able to see naked female flesh again. And unlike in the West Indies, I could touch as well as look.

It was true that Colin had given me a good screwing when we arrived here, but after a morning's proximity

137

to the other two gorgeous girls – watching and helping them strip off, then frolicking in the water with them – it was only to be expected that I'd reach a peak of randiness which had to be satiated.

'Okay,' said Colin. 'Never mind. We'll be able to use most of that and edit out the bit where you start screwing yourself. Now let's try the rest of that scene. You've come out of the shower first, had your drink, and then Sharon comes out. She's all wet, and you give her what's left of your cola. Well, perhaps we'd better get her another bottle. She won't want to drink that one after it's been up your cunt.' He scratched his chin thoughtfully, glancing over to where the other two girls were sitting chatting. 'Or maybe she would,' he added his voice lower. 'Anyhow, you two do your stuff, then Lena arrives.' He nodded towards me in encouragement. 'You're doing fine,' he said.

'Good,' I replied. I wasn't sure how I could have been doing otherwise. Today was my first day filming for Colin, but it didn't take any particular skill or talent. All he wanted was bodies, naked female bodies, young and pretty – and I fitted the bill perfectly. We didn't have to act, didn't have any lines to speak. There was nothing to go wrong – except when I got too carried away with what I was doing.

Colin shouted for order and he brought me another bottle of cola as a replacement. It was half-full, I noticed, and he muttered something about continuity. Colin was able to give us our instructions as we went along, because there was no dialogue and therefore no sound; a music track would be added later, he'd told me.

Sharon went back into the shower so that she'd be all wet again. She had a thick mane of blonde hair, but it was bleached – a fact which might not have been so obvious if her pubic hairs hadn't been jet black. Yet there was something very alluring about her two-tone design, almost like having two girls in one. Lena's hair wasn't its natural colour either, being short and spiky,

138

streaked in reds and blues and greens. Her cunt hairs were light brown, which was a clue to her real shade. She was very slim, with hips and buttocks like a boy's – yet she had enormous tits with great dark nipples, which was obviously why she'd been hired for the film. I'd hardly been able to cover one of her boobs with both hands, while Sharon's palms had been busy with Lena's other soapy breast.

'Let's go,' Colin commanded, and I resumed my position on the bench, the bottle clutched against my thigh.

Sharon appeared from the shower room, naked, shaking drops of water from her hair. She walked over and stood above me, rubbing at her breasts with her hands as if to dry herself. I passed her my cola, and she held it against her mouth, her tongue licking at the neck of the bottle.

'Good,' called Colin. 'Now put it in your mouth and let some spill out.'

The girl did as she was told, doing exactly the same as I'd done earlier. The repetition didn't seem to matter, or perhaps Colin was considering editing out the way I'd fellated the bottle.

'Good,' Colin said again. 'Now swap places.'

I stood up, and Sharon sat down.

'No,' Colin told me. 'Go behind her and start drying her hair. Lean down over her, let your tits brush against her. Good. Good.'

I followed my instructions, towelling Sharon's wet hair and bending over her, my naked breasts rubbing against her bare shoulders. She closed her eyes, her head swaying luxuriously from side to side. We carried on like this for a while, then Colin yelled for Lena. As she came in, water coursing off her nude flesh, I moved around to the front of Sharon, going down on my haunches in front of her to dry her legs. Lena stood behind Sharon, and Sharon leaned back and raised her arms to cup the other girl's big damp boobs.

I raised one of Sharon's legs, pulling her thighs

139

apart, while behind me the cameraman came closer so that he could film Sharon's pink twat. I stared at the girl's inviting cunt lips, at the tiny glistening ridge of flesh that was her clitoris, and I moved my hands higher up her leg, rubbing with the towel.

'Good, good,' said Colin, who stood close to the cameraman. 'Sharon, pour your drink down over your breasts. Lena, rub her tits. Good. Sharon, move the bottle lower, keep letting it trickle out, that's right. Now pour it all over your thatch. Good.'

The cola ran through Sharon's pubic hairs, some of it finding the shallow valley which led to her cunt and dripped into the folds of her labia, while more of it flowed down the inside of her thighs.

Without waiting for Colin's direction, I decided to improvise. I leaned forward, bending my head, and began to lick the liquid from Sharon's thighs, my tongue darting out to lap up every drop.

'Good!' Colin said in encouragement. 'Good, that's the stuff!'

My mouth moved higher up Sharon's thigh, meeting the trickle of cola, until my tongue was only an inch away from the moist lips of her cunt. I eased myself nearer, half expecting Colin to yell at me. But before he realized what I was doing, my lips were against Sharon's labia, my hands gripping her hips so that she couldn't pull away. Then I thrust my tongue deep into her cleft, rubbing up and down the walls of her vulva.

Dimly, I was aware of Colin shouting at me. Sharon twisted, trying to get free, and she shouted in protest. But I didn't care. After a few seconds of frantic licking, expecting to be hauled away from my prize any moment, I felt Sharon's fingers running through my hair then pressing against the back of my head, urging me deeper and deeper into her. The girl's hips jerked against my face as her whole body wriggled and writhed.

It had been a long time since I'd done this; and Sharon was only the second girl ever to have known my tongue. My own twat was damp, eager for a tongue inside it, and I wondered what my chances were.

Then Sharon climaxed, almost screaming out in triumph as she peaked, and my tongue lapped thirstily at the sweet mixture of cola and cunt juice. I pulled my mouth back a fraction, gently kissed her labia a final time, then withdrew and stood up, wiping my face with the back of my hand.

I looked at Sharon, but she stared guiltily at the ground and wouldn't meet my eyes. I turned towards Colin and shrugged apologetically.

He rolled his eyes in despair. 'There's only one solution for this,' he said.

'What's that?'

'You'll have to go into hardcore, that's all.'

'Hardcore?' I asked, not sure what it meant. I was still very naïve – after all I'd only lost my virginity a few days previously.

'Porn,' Colin told me. 'Films where you can fuck and suck to your heart's content – or your cunt's.'

I wasn't sure whether Colin was joking or not. I'd never heard of such a thing. Sex films were all pretence. Surely no one made movies of people actually fuck-ing . . .

Chapter Ten

Colin assured me that he was entirely serious, but I wasn't certain whether I liked the idea of actually screwing on film, or video. He didn't make hardcore films himself, although he could introduce me to someone who did if I was interested. It wouldn't do any harm to talk about it, I thought, and so a rendezvous was arranged at a bar for the following evening.

'This is Ian,' said Colin, introducing us.

We said hello, and Ian went to the bar for the drinks. He was a nondescript looking man in his late thirties, his only distinctive feature a nose which had once been broken but not properly set, casually but expensively dressed, like a lawyer or accountant on his day off.

'How's business?' he asked Colin, when he returned with the drinks. We sat in the far corner, away from everyone else.

'Okay,' Colin said, shrugging, not wanting to let the other man know how well he was doing. He'd bought a brand new sports car last week, but parked it away from the bar so that Ian wouldn't see it. 'You?'

'I survive,' Ian nodded, and I guessed that he must have been making at least as much money as Colin. He looked at me. 'So you'd like to be in porneos?' When I didn't reply, he added: 'Pornographic videos.'

'I know what you mean,' I told him. 'But I'm not sure whether I do or not.'

Ian glanced sharply at Colin.

'She's a natural,' Colin assured him. 'She just needs talking into it.'

'You get paid for fucking,' Ian said to me. 'The best of both worlds. What more could you want? There's lots of guys with big pricks. Isn't that what every girl wants?' He shrugged, as though he'd explained every-thing.

'I can't really believe that there are such films. People fucking each other? Who appears in them?'

'Girls like you,' Ian said. 'You've got a good body, so you should make the most of it. You'll be well paid, far better than you would be in most other jobs. What else could you do, huh? Work in a shop? A factory? An office? Who needs that? You only live once – so live, that's my motto.'

'But what if someone saw me?' I asked.

'That's the idea.' Ian smiled, because he was aware of exactly what I meant. 'Someone you know, that's what you mean. So what? Would you mind? I hear you've done nude photographic work, this isn't much different.'

I didn't agree. Fucking on film was miles away from posing topless for a calendar, or even making that girlie video for Colin.

'I know exactly what sort of girl you are,' Ian continued, staring straight into my eyes. 'You're the type who doesn't give a damn, nothing bothers you – you'll do anything for a dare. You're not fettered by the invisible chains which bind everyone else. You do what you want, you do it your own way, no one orders you about. You're today's girl, totally free and inde-pendent. You're young, you've got your whole life in front of you, and you ought to try everything you can – seize each opportunity, because there's nothing to lose. A moment lost is gone forever. You're the most important person in the world, and you know it. That's why you don't mind being photographed nude – you're saying to everyone: Look at me, I'm wonderful. And if they don't like what they see, tough shit. You're unique, you're you, you've got your own body, and you do with it exactly as you please. You like people to see you, to watch you. You're an exhibitionist. I've heard all about the T-shirt competition. You're at your best when you rely on your raw animal instincts and

143

lusts. You like people watching you, and you enjoyed sucking that other girl all the more because of the people who could see you. You've got so much to offer. It's the same with fucking. Society says that should be private, between two people. But why only two, and why should it be done in secret? I'm offering you the chance to fuck – to fuck as many men and girls as you can handle. No one will be telling you to stop, quite the opposite. I can simply look at you and know you'll be a sensation. I don't have to fuck you myself, I don't even have to see you in the nude. As Colin said, you're a natural. Do you want to do it?'

'I'll give it a try,' I said – because after such a sales pitch how could I refuse?

'Fine,' Ian nodded, picking up his glass of Scotch at last and draining it in one gulp. He looked at Colin. 'Ten o'clock tomorrow morning, you know where.' He stood up.

'That's it?' I asked.

'That's it,' agreed Ian.

'What about money?' I asked him.

'If you're good, and I'm sure you are, then you'll make plenty,' Ian told me, and he turned and walked away.

'You going to do it?' Colin asked, after the other man had vanished through the door.

'Why are you so eager?' I wanted to know.

'I'm only thinking of your career.' But he couldn't manage to hide his smile.

'You want to see me on screen and say to your mates, "I used to fuck her." That's it, isn't it?'

Colin took a mouthful of beer instead of answering.

'Why don't you make hardcore yourself?' I asked.

'It's a lot of hassle. Finding the right people, or any people. Problems of distribution. Anyway, when I see the guys in those films it gives me an inferiority complex.' He grinned. 'And I get jealous of them fucking all those beautiful girls.'

'But you don't mind me being fucked?'

Colin shrugged. 'You've been fucked before, you'll be fucked again. I know you can't get enough, that I'm just another cock to you. We've known each other a few days, we've both enjoyed it – but we aren't exactly Romeo and Juliet.'

I leaned across and kissed the side of his face, just above the beard.

The next day I made my first porno film.

I was very nervous when I arrived, not sure what I'd be letting myself in for, but Colin drove me to the place and went in with me. We found Ian, and then Colin left – he said he didn't want to stick around, that he wasn't needed and I could manage on my own if I just did what came naturally.

'This is Polly,' said Ian, introducing me to a fleshy brunette in her mid-twenties, dressed in a salmon pink trouser suit. 'She's the star of the show.'

We said hello to each other, and Polly eyed me suspiciously, sensing me as a rival.

'Show her the ropes, Polly, will you?' asked Ian, and without waiting for a reply he walked away, shouting to the guy who was rigging up the lights.

We were on the top floor of a large isolated house on the outskirts of the city. There was a big recreation room at the end of the landing, but it had been transformed into a bedroom, its centrepiece being a water bed. I'd heard of them, but I'd never seen one until now.

I looked at Polly, and she smiled thinly. 'Your first time?' she asked. When I nodded, her smile broadened. 'I can always tell.' She beckoned me to follow her, and we went to sit down on a sofa in the corner of the room. 'They always say that the first time is the worst, and that's probably true. I've seen dozens of girls work for only a day, or even just a few hours or minutes. But there's nothing to it if you like cock. Do you?'

I nodded, although I wasn't so certain any longer.

What if I was expected to fuck someone I didn't like? There was no reason why I had to do anything I didn't want to. I could simply get up and walk out if I wished.

Polly was still smiling secretly, as though she knew something I didn't – which was almost certainly the case, because she'd done this before and I hadn't.

'Ian's a good guy to work with,' Polly told me. 'But he expects a lot from us, know what I mean?'

I shrugged, because I didn't know.

'It's the girls who make any film,' Polly continued. 'A girl who knows her job can make the guys look really great – but the best stud in the world can only shine if he's got a girl who knows the ropes. All the guys have to offer is a few inches of hard cock. And don't believe these myths about big cocks being the best. I've tried them all, I've worked all over the world. Twelve-inch cocks? I've fucked them and I've sucked them. But they're freaks, like women with sixty-inch tits. And they're useless, believe me. So heavy that they can't even stand up straight. That's the whole mythology of sex – bigger must be better. Remember that old saying, "It ain't what you got, it's what you do with it"? It's true, believe me.'

Polly stared at me, at my blonde hair, the curves of my breasts, my long legs. She was making a point even though she was pretending to be friendly: I might be the sort of girl most guys would like to fuck, but no one should judge by appearances. When it came down to reality, I wouldn't be able to handle this film.

But she was scared of me, I realized, worried that because I was younger and prettier I was going to steal the limelight. She had good reason to worry, because I was better than her; I was better than anyone; I was better than everyone.

'You must have made a lot of these films,' I said.

'That's right,' she nodded.

'Been making them for years,' I added, smiling as though to take the edge off my words. 'I can learn a lot from you, Polly.'

She hesitated, not sure exactly of what I meant.

'You know,' I said, 'I've never seen a porno film? I'll be making one before I've even seen one.'

'That happened to me, too,' said Polly. 'So we have that in common. But of course there's a lot more being made these days. In the old days . . .' She paused, grinning. 'Before my time, you realize. They're a lot better than they used to be, better production values and plots, real motivation and characterization.'

I expected her to smile again, but she didn't; she was absolutely serious. She seemed to believe every word she was saying, as though she was some movie superstar talking about her latest multi-million Hollywood movie. But if Polly was happy in her work, then that was the main thing.

'Can you tell me something about this film?' I asked. 'What's happening? What am I supposed to do?'

'You just do what Ian says,' Polly told me. 'We filmed half of this yesterday. This is my house, my bedroom.' She gestured towards the water bed, and for a moment I thought she meant that she actually lived here; then I realized that she was discussing her film role. 'I'm all alone in bed, amusing myself with my vibrator. I've forgotten that the painters are downstairs. One of them sees me and comes into the room. We fuck. Then the other guy comes along and joins in. Usual kind of thing with two guys and one girl.'

I tried to imagine what she meant by that; I half guessed, but I wasn't totally sure.

'That's as far as we got yesterday,' Polly continued. 'Nick and Alex had to recuperate overnight. That's another thing about guys, what I was saying earlier. Once they've shot their load, they're useless.'

'Can't they fake it?'

'Fake it?' Polly laughed. 'This is the real thing.'

'But they can pretend to have orgasms, can't they?'

'There's no pretending because –' She broke off, then nodded in realization. 'I forgot, you've never seen one of these films. There's always a guy who has a real climax – he pulls his cock out and squirts his juice all over the girl. It's one of the traditions of the genre.' She smiled. 'Perhaps to prove it's the real thing, not simulated sex. In case the camera angles aren't explicit enough. Male orgasm can be faked, of course. I've seen various tricks with white of egg, but it's never the same as a throbbing cock spurting out its spunk.' She licked her lips, grinning, then put her hands on her waist. 'Sometimes I wonder if I should swallow so much come; it's meant to be very high in calories.' Then she looked at me again. 'At least you shouldn't have that problem for a while.'

'You were telling me about the film,' I prompted. I wanted to be forewarned. Two guys at once? Withdrawing and letting their semen shoot out? It sounded very intriguing.

'That's right,' said Polly, 'where was I? Oh, yes. The two guys had to take the night off so they can do it again. I think we more or less carry on where we left off, but then you appear on the scene, and they fuck you as well. You're my neighbour or something. You don't have many lines.'

'Lines?' I asked. 'I have to speak?'

'Of course you have to speak. This is a proper film, with dialogue and a script. But most of the talking is stuff like "I want your big cock in my mouth", and "That's so great", and "Oh-oh-oh-oh-oh". Ian will tell you what to say – and in any case your mouth will be full quite a lot of the time. What are you like at giving head?'

'All right, I suppose.'

'It doesn't really matter,' said Polly. 'You've just got to look as though you're good – it doesn't matter what the guy thinks. In fact, it's best not to be too good or else he'll come too quick. In movies it's mostly pretence. You've got to pretend you're getting the best fuck of your life, that whatever happens you're really enjoying yourself. When in doubt, smile. Always let the camera get a good look at what you're doing or

148

what's being done to you, even if it is uncomfortable. Let them see your tongue working on the guy's cock, let them see his shaft rubbing against your clit. You always have to keep your hair away from the side of your face, because that might obstruct the view of you gobbling away; and you've got to open your legs really wide.'

I nodded as I absorbed all this information. It seemed that Polly was being a real professional, passing on all the tips she knew because she wanted the film to be as good as possible. Or possibly she was hoping to put me off, that I might quit the set because there was too much for me to know and learn. But if I took everything step by step, there'd be no problem; I could handle it.

'Let's go down to the kitchen for a coffee,' Polly suggested, and I agreed. We got up and went downstairs, where she ground some fresh coffee and filled the percolator. We'd only been in the kitchen a couple of minutes when two men came in through the door. 'Nick and Alex,' she told me, and I looked at the two guys who were going to fuck me.

Nick was in his early twenties, Alex a decade older. Both were almost six feet tall, with dark hair. Alex wore a heavy moustache, while Nick's bare arms were both tattooed in blue and red. On his right arm a dagger impaled a heart which dripped blood, while the left showed a naked girl with a snake wrapped around her body.

'You'll see more of Nick's tattoos soon,' Polly told me, as we sat around the table and drank coffee.

The other three were talking about where they planned to go on holiday, but I hardly spoke. I didn't know what to say. We didn't have to go through the ritual dialogue the way men and women always do when they're sizing up possible sexual partners, because our fucking was inevitable.

I watched the two men, and as I did I felt a tingle in my cunt, realizing that I was eagerly anticipating what was to happen. I'd never met them before, but soon they'd both be screwing me. Or perhaps only one would have me – I wasn't sure what Ian had planned – and I tried to decide which one I'd prefer. They were both muscular and rugged, and I'd probably have been attracted to them under other circumstances. Knowing for certain that we'd fuck took away any mystery and suspense, but I could do without that. All I wanted was the basic: A few solid inches of cock . . . or even two cocks.

'Right, gang,' said Ian, entering the kitchen and nodding hello to the two other men. 'We're ready for you now. We continue with the scene where Alex and Nick are fucking Polly, so get up there and strip off. I'll be with you in a moment.'

The other three left, and Ian poured himself a cup of coffee. 'All set?' he asked me.

I nodded.

'What happens,' Ian said, 'is that you come into the room and see what's going on. You're horrified but also fascinated, watching your friend being shafted by those two guys. You don't want to watch, but you can't help it. Then you're seen, and you try to escape, but the two guys run after you; they chase you around the house, eventually catching you; they drag you back to the bedroom, stripping off your clothes; they hold you down and start to stimulate you. You don't like it at first, but then you start to enjoy it and one of them begins to fuck you while the other continues screwing Polly again.' He shrugged. 'That's the story so far. We'll take it from there, do as much as we can with two girls and two guys. Any questions?'

'Polly said something about learning lines.'

'You needn't worry about that. Anything else?'

I shook my head, even though I could think of several questions – but the answers would all be supplied if I waited to see what happened.

'Shall we go?' Ian asked, beckoning to me. We went out of the kitchen and up the stairs, pausing outside one of the rooms. 'I want you to get changed,' he told

150

me. 'What you're wearing isn't really suitable. There's some other clothes in there, things more glamorous and easy to rip off. Whenever you're ready, come on out and see what's happening.'

I went into the bedroom, closing the door behind me. I hadn't given much thought to my outfit, having imagined that I wouldn't be wearing any costume, and so I'd arrived in just a pair of sandals, loose slacks and a baggy sweater. To save time stripping off, I hadn't bothered with any underwear – but Ian had made up for that with what he'd provided for me.

I peeled off my other clothes, then began to dress up. All of the undergarments were black – a front fastening bra cut so low that my nipples weren't covered, a pair of crotchless frilly panties, and a suspender belt for the pair of sheer seamed stockings. The cotton skirt was bright red, knee-length, fastened down the right side by a row of buttons; I only buttoned half of them, leaving plenty of thigh exposed. My white blouse was almost transparent, with a plunging neckline and held together by a single bow just above my breasts, so that it hung loose and showed my bare stomach. The outfit was completed by a pair of black high-heeled leather ankle boots.

Once I was dressed, I combed my hair and checked my makeup, and I left the bedroom and went towards the room where they were filming.

I stopped in the doorway, staring at the astonishing scene. A group of men were clustered around the water bed – Ian, two cameramen, the sound engineer, and two technicians whose purpose I couldn't work out. Polly and Nick and Alex were at work on the bed. Nick was lying on his back, and Polly was stretched out on top, facing him, while Alex was above Polly. Nick's cock was in her cunt, while Alex's prick was in her asshole. And both of them were thrusting deep into her, as Ian called out his instructions to them and the cameramen.

Then the director noticed I was watching, and the

crew all backed away so that one of the cameramen could get an angle which would show me beyond the bed, watching the three performers fucking. The other cameraman came towards me as I was sent out then had to return through the door, a reaction shot made of my astounded expression. It wasn't difficult for me to look amazed, because I was. I'd never seen other people fucking, although Colin's bed had been surrounded by mirrors and I'd found it fascinating to watch myself in action from various different angles. But to see Polly sandwiched between the two men, a thick knob driving into each of her lower orifices, was a strange spectacle. I watched, my heartbeat increasing, my skin prickling with sweat. I felt timid now, deliciously menaced by the thought of Nick and Alex both fucking me.

'That's fine,' said Ian to me. 'Now we take a shot of the bed, with one of the guys realizing you're there. They both see you and chase after you. You flee out of the room, along the landing, down the stairs. But before you can get out of the front door, they catch you.'

It seemed to take ages to film the chase scene, the two cameramen taking shots from different positions as I repeatedly ran away, down the stairs, rushing for the exit. Nick and Alex pursued me, their jutting cocks like some kind of threatening weapon. They both had long thick penises, essential for their roles as porno studs. After a couple of takes, their pricks began to wilt and they had to stroke and rub at them to maintain the proper angle.

I dashed out of the bedroom and sprinted along the corridor, only arriving at the top of the stairs by the time my two pursuers had reached the door. I raced headlong down the steps, hearing the men rushing after me. Nick hurdled the rail at the top of the landing and was halfway down the steps in a single leap, while Alex took the stairs three at once. By the time I reached the hall, they were almost upon me.

Nick lunged forward, grabbing at my skirt, tugging so hard that he pulled the thing off as I twisted away, making for the door. Then Alex's hands were grasping the front of my blouse, ripping the garment from me, so that I was left with only my scant undies as covering. I tried desperately to evade the men, but it was no use. In a matter of moments they'd seized me between them. I struggled and kicked and shouted out in protest as they half-carried, half-dragged me back up the stairs, into the bedroom, and flung me down onto the water bed by Polly's side.

Polly grabbed my arms, pinning me down, while Alex pulled off my boots but kept a secure hold on my legs. Nick went to work on me, his hands exploring my vital areas, my breasts and then my crotch – and he could reach my nipples and my cunt without even needing to tug away my flimsy garments. He tongued my nipples, while his fingertips probed through my blonde curls and deep into my moist cleft. Next his mouth moved lower, lower, taking the place of his hand as his teeth plucked at the slit in my panties and his tongue thrust into my twat. My attempts at resistance diminished, and I no longer had to act, to pretend that I was being aroused – because I was.

Then Polly was bending over me, her lips pushing against mine, and I opened my mouth to admit her probing tongue – and she wasn't acting either, because there was no way that the camera could see her tongue at work against mine. She was the first female I'd kissed since Carole, and as she let go of my arms, my hands came up to caress her breasts, feeling the hardness of her nipples against my palms. She pulled her face away, her mouth closing on my right breast, gently sucking on the nipple and stroking it with her tongue. I'd never had two tongues working on me at the same time, and the effect was electric, bringing me towards orgasm more than twice as fast as a single mouth could do.

Alex had let go of my legs by now, and I felt too

weak to struggle even if I'd wanted to. He moved around the other side of the bed so that he could kiss my lips. While he attended to my mouth and Carole sucked my boobs, Nick continued to lick my cunt and softly nibble my clitoris. I began to writhe again, but in ecstasy rather than in any vain attempt at freedom.

I was aware of Ian issuing instructions, but even if I'd heard him say anything to me I wouldn't have been able to react. All I could do was lie helplessly at the mercy of the other three and their skilled tongues.

But before I could reach the ultimate height, I was left all alone – the three of them pulled away. Alex and Polly were fondling each other above me, the man stroking the girl's breasts while she rubbed the length of his prick between her hands. Then they tumbled over together, Polly on her back, and Alex plunged his cock deep into her cunt.

Nick was repositioning himself, rising up above me, then coming down, his tattooed body hugging me close, his thighs moving between mine as his prick sought for the entrance to my twat. A moment later he was inside, thrusting strongly, guiding me back towards the peak. Polly and I were stretched out side by side, as Alex and Nick fucked us. The water bed rippled beneath us.

The other girl turned her head towards me, and I twisted mine in her direction. We had just begun to kiss when I achieved my first climax, and I moaned in pleasure, my hands clutching at Nick's back. But I was unable to keep him in me, because he started to pull away. I freed my lips from Polly's mouth, staring up at the man, noticing that Alex was also withdrawing from the other girl's cunt.

They changed places, and within seconds Nick was inside Polly, screwing her furiously. Alex knelt between my thighs, his hands unfastening my bra and pushing it aside, then reaching for my panties. I raised my hips, allowing him to drag the garment off me, and I was left with only my black stockings and suspender belt. And then it was my turn to be fucked by Alex, his thick moustache tickling my lips as his face came down to kiss mine. As he pumped strongly into me I noticed Polly being shafted by Nick, his cock still warm and wet from my cunt.

Throughout this, the other three had kept talking, saying how good this was and how it was the best fucking they'd ever had. But I'd been unable to do anything apart from gasp in pleasure ever since they'd thrown me down onto the bed.

Now Alex spoke again, but it was a different kind of voice he used, more casual, not panting with lust. 'I can't hold it much longer,' he said.

'All right,' said Ian. 'Nick, what about you? Can we make it simultaneous?'

'No,' Nick replied. 'I've got a while yet.'

'Fine,' Ian told him. 'Pull out, Alex, give her it between the tits.'

I gripped Alex's buttocks, trying to hold him inside, because all I wanted was a few more strokes to give me a second orgasm. But the man pulled free, moving his legs so that he knelt astride me, his hips above my waist. He leaned down over me, holding his cock out, touching it to the flesh between my breasts. I put my hands on my boobs, pressing them together, catching Alex's prick between them as he began to rub it to and fro, to and fro. I watched as his glans retreated into the softness of my breasts, before thrusting itself forward again.

Then Alex became still, his hips pushed forward, his cock stretching between my breasts – then starting to spurt, gushing a series of hot creamy jets onto my neck and throat.

I raised my head. The spunk trickled down onto my breasts, rolling off my flesh and dripping to the bed. I reached out and took hold of Alex's cock, just below where it was sticky from the last drops of oozing spunk, and I wiped it dry with my hair. He allowed me to do it, although then he started to move away.

But I didn't want that, because of my unfilfilled desire I still needed his prick inside me. It was already losing some of its rigidity, but it was fat enough for me to rub my clit against.

'No,' I begged, speaking for the first time since I'd been brought back into the room.

'Tell him what you want,' Ian ordered, wanting me to add more lines of dialogue.

'Fuck me again,' I said to Alex. 'Fuck me again. Fuck me again.'

Alex glanced at Nick, who was still screwing his way into Polly, then he looked at me again. He sat down on the edge of the bed, then leaned back, holding his cock in one hand, pointing it upwards.

'Climb on,' he told me, 'I'll give you the ride of your life.'

I did as I was told, straddling him, my toes touching the floor, lowering my twat onto his cock, feeling it bury itself to the hilt. I sighed in delight as his hips began to rock, pushing his knob against my vaginal walls, and I clenched my cunt as he rubbed up and down, pushing myself against him.

'Soon, Ian,' said Nick from next to me. 'Where do you want it?'

'You both gave it to Polly yesterday,' Ian told him, but he was looking at me. 'So give it to her today, all over her face.'

Nick pulled his prick free from Polly's gaping twat, rising to his feet and standing on the bed, grasping his cock as he leaned towards me, aiming the glans a few inches from my face. Meanwhile, Alex was still fucking me and I could feel the build up of tension within my twat which promised imminent orgasm. Nick's hand slid back and forth on his shaft, masturbating for the final strokes towards his own climax.

We came together, my internal explosion coinciding with Nick's eruption of semen. I opened my mouth in a silent cry of rapture, and at the same time the first throw of spunk hit the side of my face. I turned my head, my hand reaching for Nick's cock, guiding it between my lips and sucking him dry in my fever of passion.

Polly slid her head next to Nick's crotch and my face, licking the length of his shaft between his balls and my mouth, her tongue sliding onto my cheek and lapping at the splash of spunk. Nick withdrew his dick from beneath my lips, and Polly opened her mouth to take him in, but before she was able, I pushed Nick aside and thrust out my tongue, showing the girl the spunk which lay in a thick film across it. Her tongue licked greedily at mine, sucking off the creamy liquid and swallowing it down.

Alex had seen Polly's eagerness for Nick's tool, and he withdrew his shaft from my cunt and offered it to her. Nick's prick was a few inches from her mouth also, and she took one cock in each of her hands, drawing them both towards her lips and sucking in each engorged tip.

All there was left for me was Polly's cunt, and so I made it mine, burying my head between her legs and shoving my tongue against her clitoris. Soon after I felt a hand on my own twat. I didn't know whose it was, and neither did I care; all that mattered was the way the practised fingers stroked my clit and rubbed against my labia . . . bringing me off for the third sensationally ecstatic time.

Finally we all lay exhausted on the bed, fingers and tongues still close to the nearest cock or cunt. If this was what making movies was all about, I decided, then it was the life for me.

'That was fine, everyone,' said Ian, and the crew started to put away their equipment.

Polly, Nick and Alex climbed from the water bed and left the room, but I continued to lie where I was, flat on my back, legs wide apart, my arms thrown out by my sides.

'You okay?' Ian asked.

I nodded lethargically.

'You did fine,' he told me. He smiled. 'Not bad for a beginner.'

But I still didn't move.

'Is there anything you want?'

'Another orgasm would be nice,' I told him.

Ian laughed. 'You're going to go far,' he predicted.

And he was right. That was my first porno movie, but it was by no means the last. Over the next couple of years I was fucked by more cocks and I sucked more of them than anyone else in the business. But it wasn't just the quantity, it was the quality of my sexual performances which brought me to the top of my chosen profession. I enjoyed every moment, each drop of spunk, all my miriad orgasms, and if I had the chance there's only one thing which I'd change – I'd want more of it!

Chapter Eleven

It seemed strange going back to my home town after so long away. The place appeared to have grown smaller, but apart from that nothing had changed. It was difficult to realize that I'd spent most of my life here, although it had hardly been living – not compared with what I'd done since.

I'd come back because of Carole. Out of nowhere, an invitation had arrived to her wedding. At first I was tempted to ignore it, simply to send her a large vibrator as a wedding present and let her make up her own mind about its implications. But after so long I was no longer angry at Carole's desertion – she'd discovered the pleasures of the penis earlier than me, that was all; and for that I envied her. It would be good to meet her again and to see her future husband, a guy called Vince.

I arrived in town the day before the wedding, and that evening I went off for a meal and a few drinks with the bride and groom and half a dozen of their friends, including a petite, raven-haired girl called Joan who was to be the bridesmaid. It was traditional for a couple to spend their last free evening apart, with friends of their own sex, but it was clear that Carole and Vince didn't want any such separation.

After Carole had introduced me to Vince and we shook hands, he kept watching me. 'I'm sure I've seen you before,' he said.

'It's not a very big town,' I told him, 'so you probably saw me around when I lived here.'

I didn't remember Vince, but that didn't mean much. When I'd lived there, I didn't have any interest in men. Vince was solidly built, like a wrestler, but his face was round and childlike and didn't seem to match his body.

Carole and I didn't have much chance to talk to one another that evening, although the few words which we did exchange reminded me how much we'd once had in common — and not just as sex partners. She'd insisted that I spend the night with her. Up until then she and Vince usually alternated their nights at each other's flat, but Carole didn't think it was proper that they should do so immediately before the wedding. Not that Vince would have been able to do much, he got so drunk that he had to be carried out at closing time and driven home by his best man.

Both Carole and I knew that her invitation to me was purely platonic. We would go to bed in the same room, but all we'd do was talk as we had up until the first time that we'd made love. Whatever we'd done was in the past, something we could both fondly remember; but there was no way we could return. We were different people now.

Even when Carole stripped off and stood naked in front of me, I merely watched her nude body with admiration, not lust. She was as attractive as ever, perhaps even better looking than a few years ago, her figure more developed. She'd been a girl when I'd known her, but now she was a grown woman; no longer with girlish ringlets, her jet black hair was curled in the latest fashion.

Carole worked at the local hospital, as an administrative secretary. She didn't know what I did, and I never told her, not because I'm ashamed of making blue movies, but because she never asked me. Had she done, I'd probably have told her the truth simply to observe her reaction.

'It's so nice to see you again,' Carole said. 'This is just like old times.'

'Not quite,' I pointed out.

'Not quite,' she agreed, grinning. 'Do you want the bathroom first, or shall I?'

'You take it first,' I said, beginning to strip off my own clothes. 'Unless you want to share it – for old times' sake.' I knew she'd refuse, and she was aware that I was only kidding.

Carole nodded, yawning. We were both tired, exhausted by the late hour and the quantity of alcohol we'd consumed. While she went into the bathroom, I lay on the spare bed. I must have drowsed, because when I next looked up Carole was standing by my side, staring down at my nude body.

'Do you think I should get married?' she asked.

'It's a bit late to ask that now,' I told her. 'Vince seems a great guy.' I was exaggerating, because I hardly knew a thing about Carole's future husband.

She was still studying me, her eyes taking in my breasts, my cunt.

'Whatever a girl can do for you,' I told her, 'a man can do better. You've got a cunt of your own, so you don't need another. But a cock, that's a different matter.'

'I know. That's what I'm thinking about. If I marry Vince, then I'll be stuck with just his prick.'

I wondered if she was joking, but her expression was totally serious.

'You only need one,' I assured her, although from my own vast experience I knew that wasn't necessarily the case. I've made films where I've taken on five cocks at the same time, in my twat and ass, my mouth and hands; I've been in others where the final scene was several knobs all gushing over my nude body at once. But for most practical purposes, one dick is sufficient. 'And you know that Vince's cock is in working order.'

'I suppose so,' Carole muttered, and she walked over to her own bed, climbing naked between the sheets. 'Oh fuck!' She sat up suddenly.

'What's the problem?' I asked, also sitting up.

'It's Vince's suit,' she told me. 'I collected it from the tailor's today, and he was meant to pick it up.'

161

'It can be done tomorrow,' I told her, as I stood and reached for my towel.

'No it can't. It's unlucky for the bride and groom to see each other before the wedding.'

'Then I'll take the suit to Vince in the morning. You're not getting married till two o'clock, so there's plenty of time.'

'Would you?' asked Carole. 'Would you go around with it?'

'Of course I will.'

'That's good,' she said, sighing and lying down again.

I went into the bathroom, and by the time I returned Carole was fast asleep.

The next morning Joan came around to supervise Carole's next few hours, starting with taking her to the hairdresser and finally making sure that she arrived at the church on time. After breakfast, I went to deliver Vince's suit to him.

After ringing the doorbell to his flat a number of times and waiting about five minutes, I was beginning to think that either Vince hadn't made it home last night or else I was at the wrong address. But finally the door opened a few inches, and Vince's face appeared. It no longer looked quite so childlike. His eyes were bloodshot, his cheeks and chin covered in dark stubble, his brown hair tangled. It was obvious he'd only just woken up. He stared at me without a trace of recognition.

'I've brought your suit, Vince,' I told him, holding up the plastic bag as evidence.

He frowned, then slowly nodded in realization. 'Oh, yeah,' he muttered. 'Thanks.' The door swung further open, and Vince disappeared into the depths of his flat.

I went inside, closed the door and followed him into the small kitchen. It was dark, and I pulled the cord to open the venetian blind. Vince groaned, blinking against the sudden light, holding up his hands to his face. He was leaning against the sink unit. I noticed his pyjama jacket was on inside out, while the pants were slung low on his hips, his pubic hairs curling over the elastic waistband.

'Want a cup of coffee?' he asked, letting his hands drop from his eyes. Then he hitched up his pyjamas to a more decent level.

'Sit down, Vince,' I told him, because he looked as though he'd fall down if he didn't. I put his suit on the table. 'I'll make the coffee. Would you like something to eat?'

'Don't mention food,' he asked, one hand rubbing his stomach and the other going to his mouth as though to prevent himself being sick. He sat down at the table. 'Just coffee, thanks. You'll have to excuse me, I don't usually get in this state.'

'That's okay,' I said, finding a jar of instant coffee, then filling the kettle, 'it isn't every day you get married.'

Vince leaned his elbows on the table, resting his head in the palms of his hands. 'I feel awful,' he said, which I'd already deduced. 'I don't think I can make it there. Two o'clock. What time is it now?'

'It's ten,' I told him. 'There's plenty of time. You haven't got to do anything much, have you?'

'Recover. My head feels as though it's been kicked by an elephant.'

'Have you got any aspirin?'

'Somewhere. On the table next to the bed, I think.'

'I'll go and have a look.'

It was only a small flat, three rooms including the kitchen and bathroom, but the last room was of a fair size and served as both bedroom and living room. I went through into there, drawing back the curtains and opening the window to take away the smell of sweat and tobacco and stale beer. The room was a tip, scattered with dirty dishes and empty bottles, dis-

163

carded clothes and old newspapers; cassettes and unsleeved records lay everywhere. The stereo was still lit up, and I located the button to switch it off. There was a television in the corner, a video recorder on the shelf below. The bed was against the far wall, its covers spilling onto the ground. I found the aspirin bottle and took it back into the kitchen, gave Vince two tablets and a glass of water, then I poured the boiling water from the kettle into two coffee cups.

'You're right,' said Vince, referring to what I'd said earlier. 'I don't have much to do. Shave, have a bath, wash my hair. Then I'll be as good as new.' He raised the cup to his lips, took a sip, and added: 'I hope.'

'Of course you will,' I said.

'How was Carole this morning?' he asked.

'She was fine. She sent her love.'

'I wonder about Mac,' he said, almost to himself.

'Who's he?'

'My best man.'

As he'd driven Vince here yesterday night, he must have been more sober than the groom – in fact everyone had been much more sober than Vince.

'I'd better phone him,' Vince continued. 'He was going to come around here later; I ought to make sure he got home okay. All I can remember is him driving me away from the bar last night, I've no idea how I got to bed.' He rose unsteadily to his feet, then sat down again.

'I'll phone him for you,' I said. 'Don't you worry about it. All you've got to think about is making yourself presentable.'

'I suppose so,' Vince agreed.

'If you want, I'll stay here until he arrives – I'll make sure you don't fall asleep in the bath.'

'Would you? That's great. I don't particularly want to be by myself. It'll be nice just to know you're here.'

'You give me Mac's number, and I'll phone him while you're in the bathroom.'

'Right. Make yourself at home. Put on the stereo if you like.'

Vince locked himself away to get cleaned up, and I phoned Mac, who said he'd be around in a couple of hours and take the groom for a couple of drinks. I passed on the first part of the message, but not the second. Then I went through into the main room, thinking of Vince's remark about making myself at home. I didn't know how he was able to live in such messy surroundings. I picked my way through the junk and looked through his scattered collection of music. After trying a few of the least dusty records, I concluded there was nothing that appealed to me and so after a while I switched on the television instead.

The set came on, but there was no picture, and I realized that the channel must have been tuned for the video recorder. I pressed the play button on the video. The television screen flickered, then settled down to show a closeup of a blonde girl fellating a sturdy cock.

The girl was me!

I watched in amazement. I'd only seen my films very rarely, I simply wasn't that interested. Once the movie was in the can and I'd been paid, it was no longer any of my concern. But now I was fascinated to watch myself in action, and I sat on the floor, leaning back against a chair to gaze at the screen.

I tried to remember the film and when it had been made, but I didn't have much information to go on yet. Just me and a prick in my mouth, but that included almost every movie I'd been in. The cock itself provided no clue, because although they varied a lot this one seemed typical of those I'd sucked throughout my career. My tongue stroked the swollen purple glans, my lips rubbing against the shaft as I drew it deeper into my mouth then let it slide almost out again.

How many people were in the film? Was it just me and one guy, or what? All I could do was sit and wait.

After a couple of minutes, my video image pulled the throbbing wet cock from my lips, the camera following it down as I aimed its tip at my right breast, and it began to spurt its seed onto my flesh. The camera zoomed in, focusing on the come as it dripped down my boob and hung from my nipple. The frame froze for ten seconds, and then the screen blanked.

I still couldn't recall which film it was, but that was hardly surprising considering the countless porn epics in which I'd featured. I pressed the rewind button, the spools spinning back towards the beginning of the tape and switching off automatically. Pushing down the play button, I watched the movie from the beginning.

As soon as it started and I saw the car, I remembered. It was one of the first films I'd made for Mark, a twenty minute short in which I appeared with another girl and a guy.

I couldn't recall the man's name, but the girl was Lena, whom I'd originally met when I'd made my one softcore video for Colin. We'd been in a number of porn films together, and her big breasts made her very popular.

In this movie we were driving along in an open-topped sports car, Lena behind the wheel. It was a summer day, and the wind blew through our hair, and we wore very little because of the heat – sleeveless T-shirts with our nipples clearly visible as they pressed hard against the thin material, brief skirts which came as high as our crotches. The camera studied our bare legs and braless breasts. We were laughing and chatting as we sped along the narrow country road, and my hand rested lightly on Lena's thigh.

As we turned a corner, suddenly there was a man on a bicycle coming towards us. Lena spun the wheel frantically, but the bike went flying into the air. The car had hit it – or so it appeared on screen. The car braked, and we both jumped out, running towards the fallen man. He was lying on his back on the grass verge, unconscious. He wore a pair of shorts and a riding shirt with the number 22 printed across it, and his peaked cap was still fastened on his head, secured by a strap under the chin.

Lena and I leaned over him anxiously, feeling for his pulse, relieved when we found it. We stared down the road, looking for assistance, but there was no one in sight for miles. We quickly debated what we should do, whether we ought to carry him to the car and drive him to the nearest hospital; but we decided to give him the kiss of life in the hope that would revive him. Lena unfastened the man's cap and bent down, tugging his jaw so that his mouth opened, then putting her lips to his. I knelt across his chest, pushing up his shirt to reveal a chest covered in a forest of dark curls, and I pressed my hands down across his ribs, as if attempting to force his lungs into action.

After a minute or so, we realized that we'd succeeded, that he was breathing properly, and we smiled in satisfaction at one another. But neither of us moved, we simply glanced down at the man beneath us – and our smiles broadened into grins. Lena resumed kissing the man, her tongue licking at his unmoving lips and exploring his mouth. I climbed off him and moved around to his hips, tugging at his shorts and yanking them down to expose his half erect cock, taking it in both of my hands and stroking it up and down until it became fully rigid. Then it was the turn of my mouth, and I leaned over his groin, my tongue darting out to meet the end of his prick, licking all around the ridge beneath the glans and finally drawing as much of his shaft between my lips as I could.

Lena was watching, noticing that I had the best of the deal, and she came over to me, pushing her face next to mine, licking at the cyclist's testicles and the base of his rod, her lips moving upwards, pushing me out of the way until at last she had his penis to herself. I backed away and stood up, looking annoyed, hands on hips as I watched the other girl tasting her prize. Then I turned my head and looked at the man. Swiftly, without raising my skirt, I pulled off my panties and

167

squatted down over the man's face, my skirt falling across his head as I slid my hips backwards and forwards.

Letting go of the saliva-coated prick, Lena followed my example, dropping her own briefs, but also removing her skirt and displaying her brown pubic curls. Then she lowered herself onto the man's cock, holding it upright as she slowly descended, the shaft vanishing into her twat. We were facing one another, rubbing ourselves against the supine male beneath us. I stripped off my T-shirt and unzipped the side of my skirt, letting the garment drop to the grass. The camera moved in to show the guy's nose rubbing against the pink flesh of my clitoris.

Now Lena also peeled off her T-shirt, and we leaned towards each other, our hands caressing each other's tits, our mouths moving close, tongues inching out to touch one another's. The camera zoomed in for a series of closeups, of our lips against each other's, of the cock sliding in and out of Lena's juicy labia, of my blonde cunt curls tickling the man's face – which was when his eyes blinked open. He didn't move for a few seconds, but then his arms slid up the side of my body, cupping my breasts.

When he'd returned to full awareness, he began to take a more positive role in what was happening, rolling Lena onto her back and fucking her while his tongue probed into my twat.

Watching myself on the screen, I began to feel my desire rising and my labia became moist. I pulled my dress up to my crotch, rubbing my pubis, then slipping two fingers inside the edge of my panties and stroking my clitoris.

On the television, I took Lena's place and the man began to screw me instead of her, while my tongue licked at the girl's cunt as she stood crouched above me. Our positions changed again, and we lay in a triangular formation on the grass. Now it was the turn of Lena's tongue to flicker in and out of my pulsing twat, while the man's mouth was locked against her cunt and he gave his cock to my lips.

This was almost where I'd started watching the film, but my eyes didn't stray from the screen as I brought the cyclist to his climax again, his spunk jetting against my breast. My breath was coming faster and faster as I finger-fucked myself, but when the screen blanked I realized that I wasn't alone.

I turned my head, and Vince was standing there. His hair was wet, he was clean-shaven . . . and he was naked, his stubby cock erect.

'I knew I'd seen you before,' he said. 'I didn't know you were a celebrity.' He licked at his lips. 'You told me earlier that Carole sent her love . . . so how about you giving me it?'

I stood up. This had happened before. When men found out that I made blue movies, they assumed I was an easy fuck. All they had to do was flash their tool – exactly as Vince was doing. But right at that moment his jutting penis was exactly what I needed.

I didn't speak, I simply pulled off my clothes and beckoned to him. Then I turned around, winding back the video two-thirds of the way to the beginning and switching it on play, and I lay on the floor in front of the television, lying so that I could watch the screen where I was tugging down the stricken cyclist's shorts and extracting his cock. It was longer and fatter than Vince's.

Vince knelt down between my legs, staring at me and muttering. He was saying how beautiful and gorgeous I was, but I hardly listened. His hands stroked my contours, rubbing at my breasts, fingering the hairs which fringed my cunt. He leaned towards me, offering his knob to my mouth. I reached out for the prick with my hand, gently squeezing and stroking it, pushing it down towards my twat because that was where I wanted it.

He got the message, shoving his cock into me, and I sighed as it slid against my cunt lips and he began to

169

fuck me. I lay almost still, letting him do it all, not looking at him but instead watching the video of my past exploits. Vince wasn't very skilled at screwing, but he was competent enough, thrusting himself deep into me, his hips swaying slightly from side to side for extra friction, grunting with every jerk of his pelvis.

It didn't take long for him to come, but luckily I was almost ready, and as his spunk shot deep into my cunt it spurred my own orgasm, and I opened my mouth and moaned rapturously. Vince collapsed on top of me, panting heavily, and I began to rock my hips up and down, rubbing my clit against the base of his shaft, bringing myself off again within a minute. By that time, my video image again had a few inches of firm cock in her mouth.

But I didn't need that now. Vince had fulfilled my requirements, and in any case as he withdrew he was totally spent and limp. I watched as for the third time the video prick squirted its gushing come onto my breast. Then I reached across and switched off the machine.

Vince watched me uncertainly from the corner of his eye, half-smirking, half-ashamed. 'Er . . .' he mumbled. 'You won't tell Carole . . .'

'Tell her what?' I asked as I stood up, feeling a drop of spunk roll down the inside of my thigh. I picked up my clothes, walked past the man and went through into the bathroom, locking it behind me. After a few seconds I heard the door handle turn, but I ignored it and stepped into the shower, pulling down the shower head and switching on a warm spray, aiming it up into my cunt and rinsing out Vince's semen.

Drying myself, I dressed and left the room. Vince was watching another replay of the video, sitting naked in the chair by the television. He stood up as I entered, turning, his almost vertical knob held optimistically in his hand.

I shook my head, smiling slightly. 'It's your wedding

day, remember?' I said. 'You'd better save that for your honeymoon and for Carole.'

Vince shrugged, then scratched his chin. 'Did you – er – like that? Was it – uh – any good?'

'It was just perfect,' I assured him, and at the time it had been. 'How about you?'

He nodded, grinning, and a moment later the doorbell rang. Vince glanced anxiously at me.

'Back into the bathroom,' I suggested. 'I'll answer it.'

Vince headed for the bathroom as I went to the door at the end of the corridor and opened it.

'Hello,' said Mac, staring at me in surprise. He didn't recognize me yesterday, so presumably he hadn't seen Vince's video – although in porn movies who looks at the girls' faces?

'Hello,' I said, gesturing for him to enter. 'I came to bring Vince's suit. He's in the bathroom. I'd better be going now.' I called to Vince that I'd see him soon, said the same to Mac, then I left.

The wedding was two hours later, and an hour after that the reception began in a hired room in one of the town's best hotels. There was plenty to eat, and far more to drink, and I made sure that I ate and drank my fill. Vince and I ignored one another, but Mac cornered me for several minutes, obviously fancying his chances; I was certain that Vince hadn't said anything to his best man about what had occurred that morning, neither had he shown the video – otherwise Mac's approach to me would have been different.

Carole looked stunning in her full length virginal white silk taffeta wedding dress, trimmed with lace. She was still wearing it during the reception, although she'd removed the veil. After the formal meal, the tables were cleared for dancing, and I managed to avoid Mac's invitation as a partner by saying that I'd eaten too much and didn't want to vomit all over him. He didn't speak to me again after that.

Joan, the bridesmaid, had a similar problem – except that she'd drunk too much champagne and really was

171

sick. Carole had taken a hotel room so that she could change out of her wedding dress before leaving with Vince for their honeymoon, and so she asked me to go up with her and help her out of the elaborate garment.

'And we haven't had much chance to talk properly, have we?' she added. 'I fell asleep last night, and this morning you took Vince's suit. Thanks for that, by the way.'

'No trouble,' I told her, as we left the room where everyone was laughing and talking and drinking and dancing. It was only then that I realized I was far from sober, but it was a positive feeling, happy and relaxed. We took the lift to the third floor and walked along the corridor to one of the rooms, going inside and closing the door behind us.

'You look really great, you know,' I said, looking at Carole in admiration.

'That's exactly the way I feel, too,' she replied, spinning around so that the skirt of her dress swirled up above her knees. 'Great. Absolutely great.'

I continued staring at her, remembering my wedding present to Vince that morning, and thinking that to be fair Carole ought to receive a similar gift. Last night I'd seen her naked, but I'd experienced no passionate desire for her body. Yet it was different now, and I wasn't certain why. I'd drunk plenty last night, too, so that couldn't be it. Perhaps it was because of Vince, that despite my two orgasms I hadn't been fully satiated. Or maybe it was because Carole was now wed, legally she belonged to another – and I ached to take her first, before Vince could consummate their marriage.

'Can you undo these buttons here?' Carole asked, turning her back on me.

I didn't move, and after a moment Carole spun around and looked directly at me. She'd been smiling before, but now her expression was serious.

'What's wrong?' she asked.

I shook my head slowly, forcing a bright smile.

172

'Nothing,' I said, 'nothing at all. I was just looking at you, remembering . . .'

'You looked sad.'

'I'm not,' I assured her. 'Not at all.' I grinned. 'I felt jealous of all those guys before, kissing the bride.'

'You shouldn't have been,' Carole said, and she came towards me, holding her arms wide, pulling me against her. We embraced, and I felt the softness of her breasts against my own boobs. I noticed a tear in the corner of the girl's right eye, and it trickled slowly down her cheek. I put my lips to her face, licking it away. Carole turned her head towards me, and our lips gently met. Tentatively, I kissed the bride.

It was Carole's mouth which parted first, her tongue creeping out and pushing its way between my lips. My own tongue accepted the challenge, thrusting against the intruder, finally admitting defeat and surrendering, caressing the invading tongue as it explored my mouth.

I was back where I'd started, so long ago; but as I lifted Carole's wedding dress, my right hand reaching up to discover she wore no panties and stroking her damp curls, while my index finger slid into her eager cunt, I knew this was another beginning.

All Futura Books are available at your bookshop or newsagent, or can be ordered from the following address:
Futura Books, Cash Sales Department,
P.O. Box 11, Falmouth, Cornwall.

Please send cheque or postal order (no currency), and allow 45p for postage and packing for the first book plus 20p for the second book and 14p for each additiona book ordered up to a maximum charge of £1.63 in U.

Customers in Eire and B.F.P.O. please allow 45p for the first book, 20p for the second book plus 14p per copy for the next 7 books, thereafter 8p per book.

Overseas customers please allow 75p for postage and packing for the first book and 21p per copy for each additional book.